Other books by the author:

What the Shadow Told Me
>(novel co-auhored with David Rachels under pen
>name of Kurtis Davidson,
>Winner 2003 Faulkner Society of New Orleans Award)

t HE Brick mUrdEr
A TRAGEDY

and other stories

KURT JOSE AYAU

LIVINGSTON PRESS
THE UNIVERSITY OF WEST ALABAMA

isbn 13: 978-1-60489-068-6 library binding
isbn 13: 978-1-60489-069-3 trade paper
Library of Congress Control Number 2011920336
Printed on acid-free paper.
Printed in the United States of America by
United Graphics
Hardcover binding by: Heckman Bindery
Typesetting and page layout: Joe Taylor
Proofreading: Joe Taylor, Stephanie Murray,
Connie James, Brittney Ivy
Cover art & design: JJ Cromer
www.jjcromer.com

The Tartt First Fiction Award is sponsored by
Center for the Study of the Black Belt, Alpha Chi,
and The University of West Alabama

Previously Published Acknowledgements:
Spawning *Roanoke Review*
Culture Clash *descant*
Outsourcing *New Southerner*
Official Friend *William and Mary Review*
Calling It Off *Red Cedar Review*
By the Numbers *Sucarnochee Review*

first edition
6 5 4 3 3 2 1

t HE Brick mUrdEr

A TRAGEDY

and other stories

For Kathleen, Julia and Leah,
my three wonderful women

Table of Contents

Outsourcing   1

Bob the Negro   12

Official Friend   48

Murray and the Holy
Ghost   70

The Brick Murder:
A Tragedy   82

At a Loss for Words   107

Spawning   128

Calling It Off   144

Culture Clash   156

Sand Castle   175

By the Numbers   182

Outsourcing

I'm not Jewish, but I'm good friends with Sammy Greenbaum, whose father is a rabbi, so when I have a religious question, I go to Sammy, since he's the only friend I have whose father is a man of the cloth. We play basketball together twice a week, MW, 6:30-8:00 at the Y, so I have to save up my moral, ethical or religious questions. Sometimes I have nothing for him. This night in May I have several questions.

"If homosexuality is such a big deal," I say, posting Sammy up, "why isn't it one of the commandments?"

"Good question," he says. "I'll ask Pops."

I get the ball, do a drop step on him, head fake him into an absurd arm-swinging jump, and bank in an easy two.

"And what's happening to the sky?" I ask.

"What do you mean, the sky?"

"You seen it lately?"

"What's there to see? It's the sky."

"It doesn't look right."

"Doesn't look right?"

"I'll show you after the game."

After we shower, we meet out front. There's not much of the sky you *can* see from out front of the Y, even on a good night. Tonight it is cloudy and there is no moon.

"I don't see anything," Sammy says.

"It's the weather," I say. "But I've been watching it, and it doesn't look . . . right."

"Well," Sammy says, "I certainly can't ask the Rebbe about something so random like this."

"You're right, I guess," I say.

We have buses to catch in opposite directions, so we usually don't stand around and chitchat.

"You just keep an eye out," I tell him, turning left as he turns right. "And remember the homosexual thing."

"Right."

That night I get an e-mail from Sammy. Terse as usual, the subject heading reads: "Rebbe sez:" and the body reads, "Your answer is in your question."

I read the e-mail with very mild interest, because by now the sky has cleared and I have gone up on the roof and seen stuff that just isn't right.

"Like what?" Sammy says when his girlfriend hands him the phone.

"Like seams?" I say.

"Seems like what?"

"No, seams."

"Like sewing seams?"

"Yes. In the sky."

Sammy laughs, but when I don't laugh with him he says, "You're serious."

"Go look for yourself."

Kurt Jose Ayau

While Sammy looks, I talk to Derishe, his girlfriend, who is way too hot for Sammy, the nerd. I guess she likes the intellectual type.

"I noticed, too," she says, whispering.

"Noticed what?"

"Stuff," she says. "Stuff going on."

"Yeah? Like?"

"Like the grass outside my building."

"The grass?"

Sammy comes back and takes the phone, but he doesn't say anything for a second, at least not to me. He whispers something to Derishe. Then he says, and he sounds kind of shook up, "Let's go pay Pops a visit."

"Now?" I say.

"The sky has seams and you're asking 'now'?" Sammy says.

"Man," I say, "when you want to, you can really put on the Jew."

I can practically hear him shrugging.

"It's a gift."

We arrive at the rebbe's house, the three of us—Derishe says she's too weirded out to stay at Sammy's alone—and all the lights are on.

"My father, he thinks I own Con Edison," Sammy says.

And I give him a snare and cymbal.

"Thank you."

The rebbe meets us at the door before we can ring.

"Your muffler is shot," he says to me. "Heard you a block away."

"Good evening, Rabbi Greenbaum," I say.

He gives me a hug. "It's such a long way that you can't visit once in a while?"

"He's busy building an empire," Sammy says.

"And when shall this beauty be my daughter-in-law and give me nice Jewish grandbabies?" he says, kissing Derishe on the cheek.

"She's Presbyterian, Pops, remember?" Sammy says.

"Hope, hope," the rabbi says.

He leads us into the living room, offers us seats, but remains standing.

"I did some research," he said. "Didn't take long."

"And?" Sammy says.

"And the news is not good."

I immediately feel guilty. It was I, after all, who noticed what was going on. Maybe if I hadn't been paying attention to things . . .

"The question is, what to do," Rebbe says.

"But what is happening?" Sammy asks.

"What's happening?" his father says, mockingly. "What's happening? I'll show you what's happening!"

None of us had noticed an upside-down glass on the coffee table. He points and we see trapped inside a housefly.

"Observe," Rabbi Greenbaum says. He removes the glass and the fly attempts to escape, but manages a flight of only a few inches before it topples over onto its side, its wings vibrating.

"What the hell, Pops?" Sammy says.

"Look closer."

And we do. The fly looks shiny and, and . . .

"Plastic?" I say.

The rebbe bows.

"The powers of perception," he says. "Plastic."

"I don't get it," Derishe says. "It can sorta fly, but it's plastic?"

"Exactly," Rebbe says.

"What's this mean?" Sammy says.

"I have a theory," Rebbe says. "But, like any good theory, I'd like to test it out before I pronounce it. Let's have some nice chicken soup, then we'll go do some tests."

The sky has seams, the grass outside Derishe's apartment is strange, and now a plastic fly. And the man wants to eat soup?

"But, Rebbe," I start to say.

"Unh, unh, unh," he says, shuffling toward the kitchen. "If the universe is falling apart, some nice chicken soup can't hurt anything."

Derishe is Cuban, Ethiopian, Swedish, Thai and Greek. Her skin is the color of honey. She has one blue eye and one green eye. I have personally witnessed three accidents on the streets of Manhattan caused by her mere appearance. I have been mindlessly in love with her for as long as I have known her, which is exactly eighteen minutes longer than Sammy has. I'm better looking than Sammy— ask anyone—and I make more money than he does, live in a better apartment and have a car, even though the muffler is, as the Rebbe says, "shot." So why am I on the outside looking in at this nectar-complexioned wonder of genetic lagniappe?

"Eh?" Rebbe says to me.

I am nudged out of my reverie by Rabbi Greenbaum's penetrating gaze.

"Sorry?"

"The soup. How is the soup?"

"Great," I say.

He turns to Sammy. "See? He says it's great."

"He's not tasting it," Sammy says. "He's worshipping my girlfriend again."

"Oh, well, I understand," the rebbe says, "beauty before soup any day."

Derishe, who has been staring out the window, distracted through this whole exchange, says in an otherworldly voice, "Are we the only ones who are seeing this? We can't be."

I'm too busy blushing and trying to hide in my soup to answer her.

"Who saw the world like Van Gogh?" Sammy says.

"Chagall?" I say.

"Excellent points, all of them," Rebbe says. He slurps the last soup out of his bowl and starts to rise, but Derishe stirs herself, stands and grabs his bowl.

"What next?" she says.

"The study," Rebbe says. "I have to feed Moishe and the boys."

Moishe is Rabbi Greenbaum's prized angelfish. Or, I should say, *was*.

"Gott in Himmel!" the old man says when we approach the huge fish tank he had his nephew the carpenter build into one wall of his study. A single angelfish is floating on the surface of the tank, and from its size and distinctive markings, we know it is Moishe.

The rabbi stands at the fish tank, his face a study in anguish writ small, looking in on the 50-gallon container, its aquatic plants, its fish. Its Moishe, dead. Sammy scoops him out with a net, lets the water drain, then gently sets the net, deceased fish and all, on the counter. Derishe puts her hand on Rebbe's shoulder and he covers it with a liver-spotted clutch of fingers.

"Such a good fish," he says sadly.

Sammy pokes Moishe's body with a finger. I notice even from several feet away that the fish's body does not respond the way it should. There is no give.

"What the heck, Pops?" Sammy says. He pokes again, then picks up the fish by its well-articulated tail. The fish is rigid.

"Rigor mortis in a fish?" the old man says.

Sammy taps Moishe against the bookcase. Tick tick tick. He sniffs it.

"Plastic!" he says.

"Oy!" Rebbe says. "The world is coming to an end! The Messiah is at hand."

I'm not very religious, but these words make the hair on my

neck stiffen.

"**M**ore light," Sammy says.

We have moved over to Rabbi Greenbaum's desk, where Sammy has pulled the magnifying glass from the boxed set of his father's OED to examine Moishe. I bend the halogen bulb lamp toward his head.

"Hmmph," Sammy says, leaning over the fish.

"What?" his father asks.

"It says 'Made in Bangladesh,' " he says.

"All this time I was telling my life story to a plastic fish from India?" Rebbe says.

"Bangladesh," Sammy corrects.

"India, Bangladesh," his father says. "When you're my age, certain distinctions don't apply."

"The fly!" Derishe says, and rushes from the room.

I will follow Derishe anywhere, so I do. Sammy and his father are seconds behind me.

"The magnifying glass," Derishe demands, kneeling by the coffee table. Sammy hands it to her obediently and she studies the fly. "Nepal."

"Nepal?" I say. "They make plastic flies in Nepal? I didn't think they made anything in Nepal."

"The world is changing," Rabbi Greenbaum says, suddenly sounding ancient, his voice a sepulchral croak.

Rabbi Greenbaum sits on his sofa sipping some cherry Mogen David wine, deep in thought.

"The sky, the grass, the flies, the fish," I say, surprising myself.

"What?" Sammy asks.

I repeat what I've just said.

"What grass?"

"My grass, outside my apartment," Derishe says.

"You didn't tell me."

"I thought I was seeing things, but then when Thomas called earlier this evening, I realized it wasn't just me."

"Maybe it's just *us*," Sammy says. "Maybe, maybe we're having some kind of, of, I don't know, Salem experience or something."

"We're all witches?" I say.

"We're all having hallucinations," Sammy corrects. He stands behind his father, biting his thumb and looking off into the middle distance. "I have an idea," he finally says, and reaches for the phone.

"Another, please," Rebbe says to no one in particular, holding out his glass.

Derishe and I both reach at the same time and our hands touch.

After half a dozen calls, Sammy sets the phone down crisply in the cradle.

"What is it with everyone tonight?" he says. "I can't get anyone."

"Are you trying home numbers or cells?" Derishe says.

"Both. It's like the whole world has gone to the movies or temple."

"It's spring," I say. "People are enjoying the city."

"The plastic city," Sammy says.

"No," Rebbe says. "Not the city. The city is man's doing."

"What are you saying, Pops?"

"Let's go out into the yard," the old man says.

"It's pitch black out there," Sammy says.

"And so why did God invent the flashlight?" his father asks.

We stand on the small deck overlooking what Sammy and I have always referred to by making quotation marks with our fingers. "The Yard," a thirty-foot by thirty-foot square of lush Bermuda grass—fanatically tended for three decades by Mr. Martinez and his sons, the best Dominican gardeners in Manhattan—a brass sundial, a trellis trailing clematis, and a small fountain. The epic whiffle ball battles waged in "The Yard" would have awed Ruth and DiMaggio. It's where Sammy and I smoked our first joint when his parents were in the Poconos and he and his brother Aaron stayed home by themselves for the weekend. The Rothstein twins provided us with our first protosexual experiences in that yard, offering their not inconsiderable breasts to our trembling hands. I could go on, but I think you get the gist of what that backyard means to us.

We stand there in the night air, the white noise of the city like a force field around us, and are silent for several seconds.

Finally the rebbe sighs and takes the flashlight from Sammy's hands. He flicks it on and a cone of light leaps into the trees. How natural do budding trees look by flashlight? Gray bark, pale green buds, a shifting shadow-shatter of branches against the eight-foot high back fence. In turn, Rabbi Greenbaum illuminates each of the landmarks that are emblazoned on our memories. He ends by shining light on the grass.

"Go, look," he says, handing Sammy the flashlight.

Sammy descends the steps, lighting his path. "The grass is looking kind of long, Pops."

"The Martinez boys are in the Dominican," the rebbe says. "They'll be back next week."

I'm right behind him on the stairs, Derishe behind me. She places her hand on my shoulder—to brace herself going down the stairs, no doubt—and my knees threaten to give out under me.

"What the heck?" Sammy says, stopping abruptly two steps onto the lawn. I stop and Derishe stops, too, but not before she bumps into me and her breasts nestle against the tops of my shoulders. She squeezes my neck and I shiver.

"What?" the rebbe asks.

Sammy kneels down, shines the light on the grass, runs his hands over the emerald green blades. Murmurs.

"Here," Rebbe says to Derishe, handing her something. She pushes me gently with her left hand and I step down into the yard too. Immediately I know that something is not right. The grass under my feet feels unlike any grass I know. It feels, in fact, like those plastic doormats with fake grass and the little daisy in the corner. Derishe steps down next to me, catches her breath.

"Oh my—" she says. A second later she hands the OED magnifying glass to Sammy.

"I knew it," I say to the night air.

And Derishe turns to me and in the wan moonlight I see her perfectly mismatched eyes appraising me in a way she never has before. Sammy is the history professor at City College, the intellectual, the scholar. I am the businessman, the dollar chaser. But I've also got an eye for the small things, an appreciation, a sense of wonder, the knack for acute observations. And she understands now. She saw it too, she told me early tonight, and now she sees something else. She and I . . .

"Indonesia," Sammy says. "The grass was made in Indonesia."

Maybe it's the scholar in him, the library grinder who can't see the big picture for all the details, but it looks like Sammy is going to go blade by blade to verify what he's found.

"What does it mean?" Derishe asks Rabbi Greenbaum without looking away from me.

"It's the end of the world," Sammy says.

"Yes," his father says. "Yes. Or it could be the beginning."

"Outsourcing," I say.

Everyone looks at me.

"What?" Sammy says.

"Outsourcing." I don't know where the words are coming from, but they bubble out naturally. "The rebbe was right. Man makes the cities, the machines, the factories, the airplanes. All the things God chooses not to do. And now God's saying to us, I'll just stand back and let you do all of it. See how it goes."

"The Lord removes His Hand," Rebbe says, stroking his beard, nodding. "Like a father says to his child, 'Fine, go ahead and see for yourself. If you wind up in jail, don't call me until after breakfast, if it's not too much to ask.' "

"Pops," Sammy says, "do you have to bring that up again?"

"The sky, the fish, the fly, the grass," Derishe says.

"Look!" I say. "The moon!"

It has burst through the clouds directly above us, full, fiercely bright. I search its surface for the reassuring features we've all known since childhood, that slightly off-kilter Mr. Bill face that you have to be a certain age to see, but instead I see taking shape two perfect circles for eyes and a watermelon-rind slice of a smile. And as we watch, and no doubt countless other millions across the world do, that ancient face that has comforted the human species for millennia slowly turns a sickening and familiar shade of yellow.

Bob the Negro

I had my suspicions. I mean, come on: the *only* black employee in the company? You know something's up with that. So I had suspicions. *Things* I thought they might be thinking about me just *because*. But I didn't have my first proof until I came in real early one morning and Stewart, the night watchman, waved and said, "Hey, Bob the—"

It sounded like he was going to say something else, like, "Hey, Bob, the heater isn't working," or "Hey, Bob, the Patriots are looking good, huh?" But no, all he said was, "Hey, Bob the—"

"What?" I said.

We had nothing to steal at Ahhh! We were a beverage company. All we did was cram our colas, citrus and berry drinks down the gullets of pre-pubescent kids. Metaphorically, of course. If someone broke in and got past Stewart and his pepper spray, they wouldn't snatch more than some computer workstations. But we had to have "a security presence"— an industrial park tenant policy—so here was Stewart, all 5'6", 220 lbs of him.

Stewart sat there behind his multiple monitors, cocking an

eyebrow.

"What?"

"No, man, you first," I said.

He looked confused.

"Me first what?"

I laughed. "I asked you 'what' first."

"You did?"

"Yeah. What, you wanna run the tape?"

We always joked about the company security cameras—they were everywhere except inside the bathrooms, top management assured us (and some of us had our suspicions about *that*)—but even the most ardent civil libertarians among us had eventually forgotten about the damned things. Now they were just a source of comedy. Any time there was a dispute, someone would say, "You wanna run the tape?" I always laughed at this line just to be polite. As a black man, I was perpetually uneasy about the never-blinking eye of The Man. I had been *scrutinized, observed, surveilled, profiled* enough in my life that it was never really funny, but I didn't want to make an issue of it, you know, *bring politics into the workplace*, because that's what people would call it. And that, for a black man, means talking about race. "There's no place for race in business," one of my business school professors had said. "The market is color-blind." "That would explain all the luxury hotel billboards in the ghetto and the Colt 45 ads in *The New Yorker*," I said out loud. That remark made me famous among the second-year students, but it also condemned me to a B in the class.

But I could be cool with the "no politics" thing. I *was* cool with it. Pops always said that black folk, like white folk, were all made different, and that we didn't have to march to the beat of the same drummer, or get our asses kicked by the same *PO*lice. Some brothers were born for the picket line and the fire hose, others were meant for the board room and stock options. Color me *Nigro latter*.

Stewart laughed and pretended to rewind a tape.

But he didn't, and I wish he had. Because if he *had* run the tape, I'd have my evidence, and most of what happened afterward wouldn't have happened. At least, that's what I like to think.

I had bounced around a bit before I landed with Ahhh!, but not enough, nor in a manner, to make someone think I was damaged goods. People job-hop for all kinds of reasons—old-fashioned upward mobility, getting scooped up by headhunters, spouse on the move, etc. Some folks, though, are just what my old management professor used to call *Bad News Bears*: serial incompetents who screwed their way up and out of jobs without somehow leaving a sufficiently stained paper trail that would alert future employers. They came in all shapes and sizes, both sexes and all races, pinheads who seemed to think that their job was done when they *got* the job, and thereafter spent their time apparently trying as hard as they could to *lose* the job they just got. The two-hour lunch men. The thirty-minute-late girls. The virus-ate-my-spreadsheet guy. Every company has a virtual hall of fame of their own *Bad News Bears*, mystery chumps ("Who the heck *hired* this guy?") single-handedly responsible for losing important clients, torpedoing quarterly performance goals or alienating regional management, then somehow, magically, moving on to a higher position in a different company.

But that wasn't my story. Ahhh! was my fourth job out of school, and each time I left a job, my bosses begged me to stay. *Begged* me. Now, I wish I could run some tape of *that*. Everybody in business, especially in M&A—marketing and advertising—likes to talk big, but that's just part of the mentality, the whole swagger and strut thing. But me? I made things happen.

Kids wearing their pants inside out? That was me at Trouble Jeans. I paid these delinquents $50 a week to make fools of themselves and before you knew it, a national trend had started and Trouble cleaned up, because we had started making jeans with pockets on the *outside* of the pants so that when our dumb-ass customers "turned," (short for "turned inside-out") they didn't have to worry about getting ripped off every time they went to the club. That got me a $10,000 bonus *and* a company Lexus for a year. Word got around.

People came *looking* for me. This last move, though, I had made out of necessity. My plan for a corporate CEO-ship had never included a stint at a regional cranberry-based beverage company, but when my grandmother got sick and had to move to an assisted living facility, I was the only family within five hundred miles, so rather than shipping her out to the coast to be near my parents, it was decided that, *if I could*, I should take a job in the area *temporarily* (she wasn't expected to last longer than a year) so that she would have some family nearby to come and visit as the end neared.

I loved my grandmother, but she seemed to grow younger each time I visited her, and the mental decline my parents had mentioned as a sure sign that she was circling the drain appeared to be an outright lie. She not only remembered my full name, Robert Adderly Wilcox III, but my birthday, the college I had attended, and the names of several of my remotely former girlfriends. So I soon realized that, barring any sudden and precipitous reversal in her condition, I might be sticking around New England for a while. That meant I needed to get real serious about making my mark at Ahhh!. It was time to get to work.

And work I did. I was in charge of the new product line, a reduced calorie drink for the active 20-something set. Deeel!ght, we called it. It tasted like flat cherry soda to me, but it wasn't my job to like the shit, just sell it. And, of course, if you were good enough you could sell Yak piss to nursing mothers. I was good enough, and my numbers were great. I never liked to take the job home with me, but whenever I visited Grandma, she wanted to hear all about what I was doing so she could "be accurate" when she boasted to her nursing home colleagues about her "favorite grandson."

"I'm so proud of you," she said one visit about two months before the beginning of the unraveling.

I always brought a couple crates of Ahhh! products when I visited. Our drinks were nutritionally sound, so the front desk folks had no problems with me handing out bottles to the residents. In the back of my mind, yeah, I thought we might pick up the contract for the home, which was owned by a leading health care consortium with three dozen such facilities, but that's not the reason why I loaded up the Range Rover with Fruit-tast!c, Berrylic!ous and other Ahhh! drinks. I did it because I loved my grandmother.

"But you got to be careful," she said, sipping some Deeel!te through a straw. She made a face. "This cherry soda tastes flat."

"It's the way it's supposed to taste, Granny."

"That's a funny way to run a soda company."

"It's not soda, Granny. They're fruit-based performance liquids."

"*Oh,*" she said, "like that nonsense they sell on tv about people sweating green and bouncing out of raindrops?"

"Something like that."

She snorted.

"What do you mean about being careful?" I asked.

"You *know* how things are," she said, making a face as she sipped more Deeel!te. *"You know how *they* are."*

Grandmother Douglass was my only grandparent from the South and, she liked to remind folks, she "had an excellent memory." "Oh, I could tell you stories," she would say, and then she would. The indignities of Jim Crow. The perfidy of a certain class of white people who just made you wait and wait and wait, wasting your day, shriveling up your life one hour at a time, just to show you they had power over you. Police dogs, fire hoses, polling booths in swamps. Lynch mobs. *The way things were.* The way things still *are.* When I was a kid, summer visits to her house would be mini courses in Black history. She would sit me down in front of the television at evening news time and ask me to count the number of Black reporters, senators, congressmen, generals, CEOs or other people of importance I saw. Then she'd ask me to total up the drug dealers, pimps, hookers and junkies I saw, and whether or not it was odd that all of these people were Black. "And just remember," she told me once, "everything you see on tv, a white man with gray hair had to say it was okay to show." For years I thought that Walter Cronkite was straight up the devil.

"These people are good," I said. "They're good people." And I believed what I said. I had worked at Ahhh! long enough to get the lay of the land. Given enough time and opportunity, bigots will always out.

"Smile a lot, do they?" she asked, and nodded toward the far corner of her double room where the television was mounted on a wall bracket. A game show was on and all the contestants, who were white, were jumping up and down on stage, smiling away.

"Is it bad to smile?"

"Well, you just remember," she said, "white people will smile to your face while they stabbing you in the guts with the knife they stole from your kitchen table."

I've been privy to some of the truly spectacular self-revelatory moments of a wide range of bigots. They will always do themselves in. Caught up in the moment (maybe two martinis too far to the wrong side of discrete), they'll do that little "are there any of *them* around?" head check, then launch into a fried-chicken-eating, watermelon-stealing, pickaninny-named-Shaquon joke that leaves people breathless with laughter or shock. Being that I'm a particular variety of Negro—Ivy League, well-spoken, fluent in three languages besides English—people will often *forget* that I'm Black. I swear! I get a little "not *you*, of course, Bob" wink, and off to the races we go. But what I'm trying to say is that this all adds up to a skill I have of judging the content of white people's character.

I usually know what I'm up against. And since I have the ability to be honest with myself, I am rarely fooled or surprised. Until, of course, Ahhh!

When you're in the middle of something, or at the beginning of a something that will soon have a middle, of which you can later say, I was in the *middle* of something, you rarely understand what's going on. My finely tuned bigotometer notwithstanding, I was only aware of a vague, well, the best way I can put it is, a vague *italicization,* a vague *something.*

There were 37 people in the regional headquarters office. I was third in command, in charge of eight subordinates. In a pinch, I could demand things of the people in other managers' lines of command, too. This is to say that I had daily contact with almost everyone in the office, whether I managed them directly or not. I knew these people. I knew how the office was supposed to run.

And things just weren't running well that day. The office rhythm was wrong. Phones rang one time too many before being answered. Replies to questions seemed to hang unspoken in the air for that extra, uncomfortable second. The cluster of people around the water cooler broke up too soon, or too late, or there was no cluster at all when there really should have been.

I attributed it to football. Both Boston College and the Patriots had lost over the weekend. After the Sox won the World Series twice, everyone wanted MORE. Victory was an expectation now, an odd turn of events for the people of New England, and so when defeat reared its ugly head now, people were insulted and downright pissy.

And then, at the end of the day, it happened again. I was leaving a little before closing because I had a dentist's appointment. Margie, the marketing support associate, had been putting some numbers together for me on pre-pubescent drink preferences on the North Shore based on some school lunch program data. I had

Kurt Jose Ayau

been expecting the numbers all day and here I was headed for the elevator before she finally called out to me and jogged across the lobby.

"Bob the—" she said, and I held my hand back from punching the elevator button.

"Yeah, Margie?"

She blinked rapidly and her mouth hung slack for a second and she looked for all the world like a vapid bikini model who had just been asked to explain the Bernoulli Principle.

"Yeah?" I said. " 'Bob the' what?"

"Oh, uh." She laughed. Pulled a strand of gorgeous honey blonde hair behind her ear. Was she *blushing*? "The numbers, Bob. 'Bob, the numbers' is what I was starting to say," she said.

"The numbahs!" I said. Everyone always got a kick out of how accurately I could mimic the Boston accent. "Gimme the numbahs!" I said.

And she did. Handed them to me in a manila folder. Mumbled something, blushed some more, then retreated to her desk. Have I mentioned that Margie was 5'4", 135 pounds of juicy, juicy woman? Well, she was, and she wore the perfect skirts for her figure, and when she walked away it was, indeed, a pleasant sight to see.

"'Bob, the numbahs,'" I said, and I hit the down button on the elevator console. I expected her to laugh and look back at me, but she didn't.

My father had what he called The Black Commandments. Commandment Number One: *Thou Shalt Not Ghettoize Thyself.* Do what you want, go where you want, screw who you want. Don't let the ignorance and animosity of others about your color determine your behavior.

Pops was an engineer back in the day when a black engineer was a novelty. People would think he was joking or telling lies when they asked him what he did and he said he was a Civil Engineer.

The stories he told about the slights he had endured at the hands of secretaries and bellhops made me mad, made us all mad. "Don't get mad on my account," he would say, "just make sure the shit doesn't happen to you." That was impossible, of course, because we didn't live on a Black Planet yet, but I knew what he meant. Control your own destiny as much as you are able. Don't be stupid. Don't narrow your horizon or your options. Recognize that basketball is not a cultural necessity, but a one-way, paved road that dead-ends at a brick wall with a rim embedded in it. Spread yourself around.

So I hung out with white kids, did white kid things, even dated a few white girls. You go through my photo albums and there are plenty of white folks in there. (Hey, Norm! How's it going, Hank?) Friends, teammates, roommates. Once I got to college the dating/sex thing was easier to pull off since the girls didn't have orders to bring every boy home to Mom and Dad. This is not to say that I've turned my back on my people. And, boy, could we get into a long discussion on *that* one. I mean, who *are* my people, anyway? Just because I'm Black am I supposed to be down with some crackhead street urchin in Abilene? Can't I just go about trying to live the American Dream, which is, basically, to mind one's own business and keep one's nose out of the business of others?

Some white people crack me up. It's like, once you become their friend, you lose your racial identity and just become another variety of White Person. *White Lite.* It's like they've assumed that you've changed sides since you've become their buddy. They'll let you into their "Nigger Confidence." It sure was a surprise to me to learn that, once I was in the club, people would just let loose. I learned much from them, learned about the unguarded moments of white folks. It was like they were saying, "Hey, Bob, come on: you talk white, you act white, you live white. You're just a black white guy."

So what I'm saying in a very roundabout way is, I should have known.

Kurt Jose Ayau

About Ahhh!. About the Bob the Negro stuff. Because that's what they were saying. That's what Stewart had let slip, and Margie had confirmed. That's what they were calling me behind my back.

Bob the Negro.

And how did I know it was "Bob the Negro," and not "Bob the Nigger"? Simple. Grandma told me so.

I hadn't intended on bringing her into this, because she didn't need the extra strain. Hell, the things she had been through in her life? The Depression, the War, Jim Crow, the Movement? My job was helping to ease her on into the great whatever with as little fuss as possible. So I didn't mention it to her. One day, out of the blue, she asked me,

"How they treatin' you at work, being the only colored boy there?"

We had been talking about all manner of shit that day—my sister Deborah and her pregnancy with her fifth child (which I thought was a tad too much, but of which Grandma approved whole-heartedly: "Can't let the Latinos pass us by! Black people have got to get back to basics!"); my parents' upcoming Caribbean cruise; the shame, the horror and the fascinating spectacle that was Michael Jackson—when she sandbagged me.

The way she asked it, so out of the blue, just caught me off guard. I stumbled, I stuttered.

She said, "Something ain't right, boy. Spill."

"It's probably nothing," I said. "I mean, there's probably an innocent explanation."

"Hmmph," she said. She sucked on a prune. "With white folks, where there's suspicion, there's a crime. Everybody always wants to be giving white folks the benefit of the doubt, just like they always want to check a colored man's story extra double hard. The PO-lice find a white man covered in blood standing over a dead body holding a knife in his hand, they gonna ask him, 'Did you see the man who did it?' And if he says, 'It was a nigger wearing a wool cap and jeans,' they'll thank him, drop him off home and haul every black man in the city into jail for questioning."

She sucked on her prune.

"These damned things don't work. I ain't been regular for three years now."

"I'm sorry," I said.

"You're one of the bosses over there, ain't you?" she said.

"I'm third in command."

"Hard enough being a black man; being a black man in charge is complicated."

Her eyes went away for a few seconds. Probably thinking about my grandfather, who had been a manager with the Boston Department of Public Works for twenty years.

"So what they calling you?" she asked.

"Well, all I hear is 'Bob, the—' "

"What you *think* they calling you?"

I laughed. "What else? Nigger. They're calling me 'Bob the Nigger.' "

"Hmmph." She stared at another prune. "There's worse things than being called *nigger*."

"Worse?"

" 'Nigger' is just reflex," she said dismissively. "First thing that pops into their minds. *Nigger* this, *nigger* that. But 'Negro,' that's something they think is *funny*. They been *thinking* about that. They think it's funny and they're laughing at you every time they say it. You they little joke, *Bob the Negro*. 'Nigger' is hate, but 'Negro' is disrespect. That's what they calling you."

And then she laughed.

"Thanks," I said.

"What you gonna do about it?" she asked.

"Make them stop."

"You got any proof they saying it, other than them slipping up a few times and saying, 'Bob the—'?"

I shook my head. She snorted.

"I'll get my proof," I said.

"Here," she said, handing me her bag. "Have a prune. If you're anything like your grandfather, you're gonna need these."

I didn't want to think that the nickname was all that widespread, to make a generalization about the entire company based on Stewart and Margie. So I feigned ignorance and went about my business. After all, there was work to be done. Cranberry-flavored drinks to foist on every available young athlete or spectator of athletes in America.

But it was as though a mental Ebola had infected the company. I would approach an office and hear someone say, "Hell, get Bob the—" and then silence as I walked past. Looking in, I would see a Munch canvas of frozen, guilty faces.

"Hey, what's up?" I'd say, and people would murmur something meaningless. Caught. Caught on the downstroke, in that guilty place where suddenly pleasure is short-circuited by surprise and guilt.

Soon I imagined that conversations not even remotely about me somehow got bent my way by some inexplicable force, that people became incapable of *not* talking about me, that my dark visage overwhelmed the consciousness of these good folks, put a muscled forearm against the carotid artery of their imaginations, and made them, on the pain of passing out, diss me. It was a strange time.

My grandfather was infamously irregular, a tightly-strung, anal-retentive, compulsive man. As an engineer with the Department of Public Works in Boston, it was Grandpa Douglass' job to keep the shit flowing smoothly, as he liked to say. Sewers, water mains, gas lines—when they were running fine, no one went looking for Grandpa D. But when a water main on Commonwealth Avenue broke in February, it always happened to be Gramps who was on call. There were other engineers on duty, but he was the one who always got the assignment. "That's just the way it was for a colored man back in the day," he'd say. "I didn't complain. I had a job and I wasn't getting fire hoses or police dogs turned loose on me."

My mother said I inherited my drive from him. When she would find me still up at 2 a.m. when I was in high school retyping a project due the next day, she'd say, "Just like the Old Man."

Like Grandma said, I inherited his digestive system as well. Which is why once the 'Bob the—' shit broke, my insides damned near shut down. So it was a matter not just of pride that sent me on my mission of uncovering the culprits, but of being able to take a decent shit.

I'm no techie, but I figured that the tech route might be the only way to get to the bottom of this. After all, if everybody was in on it, whom could I trust? The thought did cross my mind that Margie, JuicyJuicy Margie, might be the weak link, that she might be susceptible to my charms and be my eyes and ears, but that would take time, and time wasn't on my side. In addition to the whole regularity issue, there was the new campaign for our first entry into the alcoholic beverage market, our cranberry/vodka/cinnamon spritzer, Vo!la!, that had to be launched. Vo!la! was all mine, and I was going to deliver. So I had to get back to some sense of normalcy.

My best friend, Ruley, was a software project specialist with BankNow's headquarters in downtown Boston. His 25-man crew of nerds and technicians kept the bank's 24/7 e-banking operations running. If there was a technical way to answer the question, Ruley would know it.

"Simple, my Negro," he said, laughing as I scowled at him. "I'll set you up with some wireless mics and you'll have that place under surveillance doublequick."

"That's great. Is this, uh—"

"What, legal?"

"Yeah."

He just gave me *The Look.*

"I'll call you in a couple of days," he said.

Later that week, under the pretense of working late one night, I set up my series of microphones. There was no need for cameras. I wasn't trying to catch anyone stealing anything; I just wanted to hear what they were saying. Unless, like Ruley said, people were *pantomiming* "Bob the Negro," images would be unnecessary.

I had to be extra careful. Remember, we already had our own surveillance cameras everywhere, so I had to go into *Stealth Negro* mode. My best move was how I got some microphones into the ladies' room. The men's and ladies' rooms are right next to each other, and there's a camera right outside for the express purpose of catching perverts going in the wrong door.

First, I went into the men's room and waited three or four minutes, then came out with my face and hands obviously dripping water (telegraphed message—*There are no damned towels in the men's room*!), shook myself vigorously, and, after much *obvious* soul-searching, and feeling *visibly* uneasy, I quickly ducked into the ladies' room for some towels. Bam bam bam, teeny monitors in the ladies' stalls, snatch some towels and out I came. Total elapsed time couldn't have been more than twenty seconds. I came out with a handful of towels, rubbing them vigorously on my face and hands. I looked up at the surveillance camera and shrugged sheepishly.

Then I played it relaxed, did my job, ran my meetings, took my calls, visited the field testers, all that. Didn't show a trace of suspicion. Went out of my way not to surprise anyone in what might turn out to be a conversation about me. Whistled as I walked down the hallways. *Here Comes Bob the Negro! Y'all best quiet up!* And no one was the wiser.

"Guilty? You feel guilty?" Ruley said. "Brother, these are the people who are doggin' *you*, disrespectin' *you*. You know where this shit leads? It leads to you gettin' passed over for that juicy promotion, that glide path to the top job, because once they start talkin' about you like this, they start reinforcin' *feelin'* about you like this, and that means your cred is shot to nothing, man."

"I'm not going to be with Ahhh! forever. This is just temporary."

"Old people can fool you, brother. Grandma might hold on for another ten years, and if the economy goes south and you *need* to be at Ahhh!?"

"Things would have to get real, real bad for me to be stuck there."

"Well, just keep the guilt in reserve for when you really do something you're gonna need to feel guilty about. Because right now? You a righteous brother on a holy quest. And you're not just doing it for yourself." He got that Martin Luther King quaver in his voice. "Just remember: you're doing it for alllllll the Bob the Negroes coming after you, too."

"Aw, fuck you, man!" I said, and Ruley just laughed.

Each dime-sized microphone, affixed with adhesive practically anywhere, was powered by a hearing-aid-sized battery. They transmitted on an ultra low frequency to a digitally-encrypted "black box" I kept in my desk. The "black box" recorded data onto a removable micro drive that I swapped out at the end of every day. I took the drive to Ruley's and he downloaded the day's worth of conversations to his hard drive, digitally decrypted it, and we listened.

It didn't take long to hear what we were after. In fact, it happened so quickly that Ruley said, "Damn!" and couldn't stop laughing.

It was Jeffers Heathfrisch, the finance officer, sitting at his desk early Tuesday morning going over his daily schedule. He mumbled about the various tasks he had to perform, talked to his computer as he surfed the web, took a phone call, then went back to his schedule. He then said,

"Eleven o'clock. Management Team meeting. Tony Everson, Mason Hartwood, Bob-the-Negro, Margie Margie Margie." When he said "Bob-the-Negro," he said it haltingly, in a singsong voice, like it was a little song. Which, in fact, we soon learned, it indeed was.

"That's one," Ruley said. "Day hasn't even officially *started* and we have our first documented incident of downright dirty disrespect." He pulled his glasses down to the tip of his nose and looked at me over the frames. "And you know what this all means, don't you?"

"That people are playing me for a fool?"

"More like they gonna be *paying* you like a fool. This is *surefire* discrimination! This is what my lawyer friends call 'actionable,' Yo. This is money, bra."

I couldn't care less about money. I was humiliated. I should have saved some of my indignation, though, because we had a whole day's worth of listening to do.

"This is going to take forever," I told Ruley. "We got thirty five employees to listen to."

Ruley snorted at me. His fingers attacked his keyboard.

"Have faith in the master's skills," he said. "I've got some filters I will apply. Coupla this." Tikka tikka tikka. "Coupla that." Tikka tikka tikka. "And we done."

In rapid succession I heard a dozen people call me Bob the Negro, many of them laughing, but some just deadpan, like it was something they said and heard *all* the time, like it was something they had been told to do.

"Shit," Ruley said, "this is worse than I thought. No telling *how* long this has been going on."

The proverbial straw, though, was Margie. Margie singing.

Singing the *Bob the Negro* song. It didn't have any lyrics other than those three words, but it had a rather complicated melody. And while she was singing it, two other people came up and started singing—started harmonizing!—with her.

"Man," Ruley said. "You know what you got to do now, don't you?"

"What?"

He got this weird gleam in his eye.

"Shit, brother, you gots to kill 'em, kill 'em all. I know a couple roughneck niggaz from Roxbury who'll do 'em all for $200 and a couple buckets of Popeye's."

"Let me run to my ATM," I said, and Ruley laughed so hard he had spittle rolling down his chin.

We kept listening. The worst was these two guys in shipping. I remembered the situation. I had approached them from across the warehouse. As they saw me approach, they had held what appeared to be a conversation, but which was, in fact, just them saying "Here comes Bob the Negro, Here he comes walking in a Negro fashion, Walking Negro, Bob the Negro, Bob the walking walking Negro" in a Bill-Murray-Saturday-Night-Live-sleazy-lounge-singer fashion. And then I heard myself calling out to them and they were *still* singing, seeing just what they could get away with, I guess, how long they could go before they ran the risk of me hearing them. We talked for about thirty seconds—I needed something sent to Buffalo early next morning—I said goodbye and the one guy, Brandon, said, "Okay, see ya, Bob . . . the Negro." He waited about three or four seconds. I couldn't have been more than fifteen feet away. And he said it loud enough that you'd think that I had heard him. And this was obviously after I knew what was going on, so I was listening for people to slip up, yet still, somehow, he pulled it off.

"You heard enough?" Ruley said.

"Too much," I said.

"Sorry about that, brother. This is some wrong shit."

"Margie," I said.

"She the juicy one you been telling me about?"

"Yeah. Man, she was singing the song."

"But she sang it kind of tenderly, I thought."

"Fuck you, motherfucker."

"No, I'm serious. I mean, to her it could just be a song. No harm meant. Just like a mindless ditty that she sings. It means she's thinking about you."

But I didn't want to have anything to do with Ruley's theory about Margie, or with Margie herself or with **Ahhh!**. I was just glad it was the weekend, because if I had to see those people the next day, the next time Ruley saw *me* it might very well be on CNN in a slow speed chase with cop cruisers following me down the Turnpike after I had gone *OFF* on my fellow employees at New England's most promising new beverage company.

"Ain't no other way but all the way," Grandma said. "You push, they gone push back; they push back, you gots to push back harder. Only one place it all ends up, because they ain't gonna let you 'get over' on them, or whatever it is you young folks say these days."

"It's not about 'getting over,' it's about what's right."

"Since when that stop white folks from doing what they want when they thought nobody was watching? Hmm?"

Grandma's essentialist arguments often chafed me, but I had to respect her views because she was my grandmother and because, as she often put it, she'd spent "a whole lifetime watching the stupidity of white people." She had the scars to prove it.

"Grandma, all white people aren't bad."

"Of course not! I never said such a thing. But when certain things line up, like they lining up with you, you best just make up your mind—all the way, or get out of the way."

This was the Sunday after Ruley and I had spent most of the

day scrounging around in his raggedy apartment for something to appease the munchies. I hardly ever got high any more, but this was a special occasion, I kept telling myself. Now I was telling myself that smoking angry was a bad idea. I felt limp and paranoid and itchy.

"There's a whole lot of shit white people can get away with. Well, basically anything. Genocide. Medical experiments. You name it. So if you're gonna fight—"

"Go all the way?"

"Ain't no question mark about it, boy."

Grandma was right, but I wasn't going to get all militant, go "Ghetto Ass" on Ahhh! as Ruley suggested. I had to think about my future. And it wasn't about money, either. There are plenty of black folks out there who think that the legacy of slavery makes it legit to use any excuse to get money from The Man—but I'm not one of them and never have been. I only want the chance to earn something, and then the right to keep what I've earned.

Rather than just going right to the top, to Dirk Solaire, the Regional Manager in the downtown Boston office, I decided to start right where I worked. A way, I suppose, of letting people come clean on their own. Maybe if my co-workers knew that I knew, knew how much it hurt me, they would just stop. I wouldn't even need an apology. All they had to do was stop.

So I made my third mistake and talked to Jim Drexler, who was a team leader like I was, except his area was finance.

We had lunch.

"A song?" Jim said. "What kind of song?"

I hummed him the melody as best I could remember it.

We were eating at the new Japanese noodle place in the mall. He kept his head over his soba bowl as he scooped noodles into his mouth with his chopsticks.

"Doesn't ring a bell," he said, shaking his head. He slurped some broth, Japanese style. "You say people are singing a song about you?"

"Well—" I said.

"How you know it's about you if you don't know any of the lyrics?"

"It's—it's just—I don't know. A sense I get, you know? I hear people singing it when they don't know I'm around, and when they see me, they suddenly stop."

"Hmmm," he said. Slurp slurp slurp. "Well, I can't say I've ever heard it."

"Okay," I said. I wanted to believe him, but he wouldn't make eye contact with me for the rest of our lunch hour.

Before we headed back to the office, Jim went to the restroom. I waited for him in the parking lot. And I would swear that I heard him whistling *Bob the Negro* as he came across the hot asphalt toward me.

"Let's go sell some sugar water," he said, climbing behind the wheel of his Hummer.

I realized my mistake almost immediately, but not the enormity of it until later. When we got back from lunch I could feel thirty-six pairs of eyes watching me at every opportunity. Conversation, bubbling like a rich fountain seconds earlier, would sputter to an embarrassed silence the moment I entered a room. And then people would cough, look at their watches, scratch the backs of their necks and find pressing business elsewhere. When I approached Margie's desk to ask her a question, she grabbed her phone, held up a finger for me to wait, and then proceeded to go through a series of "Uh huhs," and "Yeahs," and "Mm hmms," until I gave up and went away, but not before I noticed that none of the lines on her phone console were lighted.

Ruley just laughed at me over the phone.

"What you expect? They all gonna say, 'Aw, yeah, you right,

you right. We been making fun of your black ass for two years now and you caught us so we're just gonna kiss your butt now and admit that we been bad'?"

"I just can't believe it," I said.

"Well, damn, Niggah, I guess you just gone have to find out, ain't you?"

Dirk was an Olde New Englande Ugly kind of guy—rich with fucked *UP* teeth and a broken nose that kept you wondering why he never got that shit fixed. William F. Buckley ugly. Conan O'Brien ugly. I mean, he was pulling an easy mid-six figures. Orthodontists and a good plastic surgeon could have fixed him right up. But it's like those portraits you see of ruling families from the 18th Century and whatnot—ugly as sin on a bicycle and wanting the whole world to see it. Like saying, Yeah, I'm *that* rich. Dirk could have been a duke or viscount back in the day.

"Really?" he said, his head popping back like I had snapped a rubber band under his nose.

"I have proof," I said. I slid him a copy of one of Ruley's flash drives.

At first Dirk looked at it as though it were an infectious turd and he was trying to remember the OSHA emergency hotline, but then this look passed across his face, this complicated look of surprise, recognized opportunity, suspicion, elation, fear, and some other things I can't quite put my finger on. Like I said, it was complicated.

"Do you mind?" he asked, tentatively reaching for the stick.

"No, go ahead."

He picked it up between thumb and forefinger and then, like an old time magician, flipped it across his knuckles as though it were a quarter.

"All right," he said, nodding decisively. "I'll look into it."

"Thanks, Dirk," I said.

He winked at me, made a little clicking sound with his mouth. "Don't mention it, pardner."

But it's a beautiful day out, Grandma."

She sat in her bed and shook her head.

"I don't have no time for you today," she said.

"What?" I was stunned. "No time for me?"

"You gonna play the fool, you gonna play the fool by yourself. On your own time. You don't need to be wasting old folks' time with your foolishness. What little time we got left, we don't need wasted."

"But I—" She cut me off with a raised hand. "I did what I thought was right," I said, but it was like speaking to a concrete wall.

The next day someone's car was parked in my spot. I figured it was a salesman who didn't know any better, so I didn't ask Stewart at the security desk to page the numbskull to come down and move his Buick Park Avenue.

As I moved through the office, people avoided eye contact with me. When I got to my desk, my computer was gone.

"What kind of shit?" I asked no one in particular. The rest of my stuff was all there, but the work station and my monitor were gone.

I called Margie.

"They took it this morning," she said.

" 'They'? Who, 'they'?"

There was a pause and I could tell that she had cupped her hand against the mouthpiece.

"Who, 'they'?" I said again when I heard her breathing.

"I—I can't tell you."

"Can't tell me? What the hell—?"

"Someone will be by in just a minute." And then she hung up.

I poked my head out of my office and I swear I could hear people snapping their heads back behind their cubicle walls.

I suddenly had this sensation of seeing myself from one of our surveillance cameras, a kind of bootleg out of body experience, a DuBoisian moment of double consciousness, because I wasn't dying or anything, just standing there wondering what-the-fuck-in-hell was going on. I heard someone coming down the hall. Singing.

It was Dirk.

"Hey, Dirk, somebody took—"

He held up his hand.

"Let's talk in the conference room, Bob—okay?"

And I swear there was, like, this half-second pause after he said my name. Like he wanted to say it.

"Say it," I said.

"What?"

"Go ahead. Say it."

"Say what?" he said, looking very confused, convincingly so, I might add.

I could feel myself getting hot and angry. The kind of angry I got only on the basketball court when things aren't going well—either I'm shooting like shit and the person guarding me is talking trash, or we're playing one of those nutjob guys who's always questioning the score and calling cheap fouls and double-dribbling and it's just driving me crazy—and this mounting anger becomes this organic thing that I can't stop. I even have these out of body experiences where a part of me is watching and shaking my head at what the other me is doing. It's a wonder I haven't killed anybody yet when I'm in one of those moods.

Dirk was still giving me that confused look.

"Whatever," I said.

He turned and headed down the hallway.

There were two other people in the conference room. Linda, one of the battle-ax older secretaries who had been with the company forever, sitting there with a little stenography machine in front of her, and this guy I didn't recognize at first. But then it came to me. One of the lawyers. Shit.

Dirk sat at the head of the table. He motioned for me to sit.

"For the record," the lawyer said, "this is the termination hearing for Bob the—, for, uh, Bob Wilcox."

"Termination?" I said. "What the hell are you talking about?"

Linda's hands were moving stealthily across her little steno machine. I turned to Dirk, but he wouldn't make eye contact.

"I am presenting Mr. Wilcox with a copy of the terms of employment contract he signed when he first was hired by Ahhh!" the lawyer said. "Mr. Wilcox, do you recognize this document?"

I just stared at the sheaf of papers he handed me.

"Mr. Wilcox, you may answer by speaking or merely by nodding or shaking your head."

I nodded.

"Let the record show that Mr. Wilcox has affirmed recognition of the contract by nodding his head."

Linda's hands flew.

The lawyer was talking again.

"All the way," I heard him say.

"What?"

"Look all the way through the document and acknowledge whether or not that is your signature at the end."

"This is ridiculous," I said, but I leafed angrily through the papers anyway. "Absurd. This is so fucking outrageous. *You* are the people who are in trouble, not *me*."

I reached the last page, saw my signature and the date, and suddenly realized that I had spent much longer than I liked to remember working for this two-bit company.

"Naw," I said. "That's not my signature."

"You deny that the signature on the document is yours?"

"Nope," I said. "My name isn't Bob Wilcox. Everybody knows

it's *Bob the Negro*."

Dirk looked momentarily embarrassed. The lawyer looked at Dirk and Dirk made a little "proceed" gesture, rolling his finger.

"If need be we can establish that this is your signature with handwriting analysis."

I shook my head. The lawyer was talking like a punk. Like one of those double-dribbling, calling-pussy-ass-fouls punks.

"I'm going to have the NAACP, the ACLU, the SCLC and the Urban League so far up your asses—"

I searched for the proper metaphor, but nothing came to me so I simply said,

"—jive fuckasses."

Linda's hands were a blur.

"What the hell can you possibly even dream of firing me for?" I said, giving the lawyer my best Negro Terror Staredown.

He opened his mouth to answer, but the conference door opened and an elderly black man wearing a yarmulke bustled in, or did his best impression of a bustle. When I say he was old, I'm talking about my grandmother's age, from the looks of his bent shoulders and awkward, hip-swinging amble. His closely cropped, tightly curled hair was snow white and his eyes behind his thick glasses looked the size of golf balls. A dusting of whiskers dotted his chin and jaw, even though it was only nine-thirty.

It was Hobart Johnson.

The Hobart Johnson, a legend among black business folk. He was the first prominent black managerial hire by an American corporation. IBM had made page six of the *New York Times* with the announcement that Hobart had been made Vice President of Human Resources in 1951. Since then he had held that exalted position aspired to by all black businesspeople in no fewer than 32 Fortune 500 Companies. He was known to the readers of *Black Entrepreneur* and *Black Business Professional* as TONICA—The Oldest Negro In Corporate America. He was known, but he wasn't necessarily admired or respected. In fact, many people called him the Black Anti-Christ for the positions he had taken on behalf of corporations and against black workers. As often as not, when you saw Jesse Jackson at the negotiating table with an American corporation, TONICA was his counterpart on the other side of the mahogany, his lantern-jawed, implacable stare into the camera as he shook hands with Jesse over those wide tables and crystal water carafes glistening with condensation a statement of righteous corporate resolve. TONICA was the rock upon which corporate intransigence against Black people was built.

No one could deny the powerful life story that made him a living legend. He was the product of the toughest streets of Southside Chicago; a World War II veteran of the 961st Tank Regiment, the first American troops to cross the Rhine, the Black Panthers, as they were known; winner of two Silver Stars for conspicuous bravery, a Bronze Star and four Purple Hearts. He carried enough shrapnel in those old bones that he was known to shut down entire airports when he passed through security. Some black business people said that TONICA was the best thing to happen to African Americans in corporate America since A. William Randolph and the Pullman Porter Strike. He helped clean out the deadwood, the riffraff, the unqualified, the Equal Opportunity Squatters, who, once they slipped through the side door, managed to stay ensconced in a company, regardless of their qualifications or skills, like arterial plaque that no amount of statins or angioplasty could remove. He made black people earn what they got, so he raised everyone's standards. To others, he was simply the 21st century face of Booker T. Washington, the accommodationist, the go-slow Negro, the Black Judas. Whatever others thought of him, I knew one thing: he only showed up when it was time for someone to get their black ass kicked, and the only black ass available for getting kicked today was attached to *moi*.

He was a man nearly as wide as he was tall and his head was a rough-hewn rectangle. Everyone got up when he entered the room. He nodded at us all, gave me a squint, then slapped down on the conference table a leather valise that looked like he had used it to smash open Nazi skulls 65 years before. Sitting with a grunt in a chair that groaned beneath his weight, he looked around the room and asked, "Where's Jesse?"

Dirk and the lawyer and Linda laughed and I almost did until I remembered this man was here to ruin my life.

"Bob, Mr. Johnson is here as a friend to the Corporation. We want to conduct this business with as little acrimony as possible and thought that his presence here would—"

"Intimidate me?"

TONICA set his jaw. I could see the ghosts of dead Nazis in his eyes, the spirits of all those goldbricking Negroes through the years he had displaced from the bowels of corporate America like a powerful high colonic.

"I haven't done anything wrong!" I said. (And I wondered, in passing, if stenographers used exclamation points, or if they wrote things like, "yelling and waving arms.")

TONICA grunted and ran a dry hand along his lower jaw, the sound like someone sanding down a piece of rough wood. He pointed to the sheaf of papers in front of me.

"You look at the papers, son? When the man gives you papers, you got to look at the papers."

I was flummoxed.

"It's the employment agreement I signed. So what? I've signed them before."

My phone vibrated then and I checked it. Ruley had texted me: "??" "TONICA," I typed back. Ten seconds later came the reply, "RIP, BTN." I turned the phone off.

"So you're saying you're comfortable with your level of familiarity with those documents not to have to read them at this time?" Dirk said.

Kurt Jose Ayau

"If you guys have a lawyer, shouldn't I have a lawyer?"

He shrugged. "I don't think it is necessary at this point."

" 'This point'?"

The lawyer said, "You are not being asked to sign anything now. You are not obliging yourself to anything."

"You're simply firing me."

"That is one of the words in our secondary documents, yes," the lawyer said.

"Like Negro?" I said. "Or is that a primary document word?"

No one said anything. TONICA squinted at me.

"Bob, Bob," Dirk said, "this is not the time for recriminations and anger. We've just decided that it's time for you and Ahhh! to pursue different opportunities."

"Firing me over what?" I said.

"Theft of corporate property," Dirk said softly.

"You're kidding, right?"

Dirk turned to TONICA, who said to no one in particular, "Let's run the tape!"

The lights went out, and the ceiling projector illuminated a built-in wall screen with a low-definition black-and-white surveillance camera feed. It was my office. The time stamp in the lower right portion of the screen established the date from six months ago.

The lawyer narrated. The secretary typed.

"As the surveillance film will show, on April 28th, 2009, Mr. Wilcox removed Ahhh! corporate property from the premises for his apparent personal use."

I watched the video, which had been spliced from several cameras over the space of half an hour. Yup. There I was, taking a stapler home with me. I picked it up off my desk, slung my laptop case over my shoulder, turned out my lights, and left my office. Then I walked down various hallways, saying goodnight to people. I even stopped in Jim's doorway and spoke using the stapler as a prop. I pantomimed stapling things together. The tape continued, following me to the elevator, where I waved to the camera with the stapler, then into the lobby, out the front doors and across the parking lot.

TONICA grunted.

"Fast forwarding through Ahhh! corporate surveillance tapes, we do not see the return of this stapler, though, we can imagine, Bob the—Mr. Wilcox had ample opportunity to do so. Instead, we see this."

More surveillance tape, time stamped just three weeks ago. I go into the supply room and rustle around in some drawers, finally producing—suspense heightens!—a stapler, which I take back to my office. The tape ended. TONICA grunted. I laughed.

"That's it? That's all you've got? You're going to terminate an employee whose gotten outstanding reviews seven quarters in a row over a stapler I forgot to bring back?"

TONICA leaned forward onto the table and steepled his hands. He cleared his throat, then spoke slowly.

"Young man, young man." His baritone made the air around my ears vibrate. I was caught between the conflicting desires of wanting to observe this relic of Black History in action and wanting to flee. "I converted to Judaism in May, 1944. You know why?"

I looked to Dirk as if to ask, "What the fuck?" but Dirk was watching TONICA.

"No," I said to the old man, "why?"

He unsteepled his hands, clenched them around an invisible throat, and spoke in an increasingly precise and menacing tone: "So that when I sent those Nazi (he pronounced it the way Roosevelt does on those old newsreels: 'Nitsi') motherfuckers to hell, the last thing they saw was a nigger wearing a Star of David!"

So quick I almost missed it, Dirk made a motion for Linda to stop typing.

The lawyer removed his glasses and cleaned them with the tip of his tie.

I laughed in the old man's face.

"What the hell does that have to do with anything?"

"You're a little thief, you common nigger! A common nigger thief!" He stared at me, trembling. "You think the Nazis are afraid of—of common thieving niggers? Do you? Well, they aren't! They aren't afraid of you at all! You little thieves from, from Mobile, from Shreveport and Appalachicola and, and Baltimore!" He waved his hand across the tabletop, a giant cleaning the map of negro dross. "They'll just laugh on their way to hell."

Silence blossomed in the room like an evil flower. TONICA's hands came to life as he grew more animated.

"Why, back in the slave days, a thief like you would have the master beating all the slaves down in the quarters! The women, the children! A piece of ham missing? Whip them! Some cornbread unaccounted for? Tear their flesh from their bodies with a cat-o'-nine-tails!"

He had risen from his seat now, albeit slowly, and though he stood towering over me, I was fairly certain that if I needed to, I could drop him with one good shot to the jaw. I was ashamed of myself as soon as I had the thought, but I was still ready to do it. Calling me Bob the Negro was one thing. But a thief?

"Step to it, old man," I said. "I'll lay you out like last week's drawers."

"Mr. Johnson," Dirk said gently. "Mr. Johnson."

And the old motherfucker turned that rectangular head around like he was a robot or something, a Nazi strangling android. He looked confused.

"Sir?" he said to Dirk.

"Thank you," Dirk said.

TONICA grunted again, rubbed his face, gave me a stern look, and sat back down.

I stared at Dirk, held my hands up: *What the hell?*

"I think we're done here," the lawyer said. "I think we have all we need."

And just like that it was over, my career at Ahhh! done. They had gotten me. Gotten me good. I could have appealed, gotten a lawyer of my own, made a big stink about the race issue and all that, but they had me on tape threatening this icon of black business longevity. Linda had conveniently not recorded the decrepit bastard's mindless ranting, but had started up again just in time to record me saying, "Step to it, old man. I'll lay you out like last week's drawers." TONICA, though he had sparred with the NAACP and the Urban League, was still a respected black figure, and if it came down to a young punk like me and a "legend" like him, who do you think was going to lose? No civil rights group would touch me.

I was at least given the dignity of not having a security guard watch over me as I packed up my shit. Still, I knew I was being watched, and that if I tried anything "funny," they would be on me in a heartbeat.

I'm not a big memorabilia man like some guys who have their wall of photos with pictures of them smiling like a jackass next to a series of celebrities, but I did have mementos from previous successful campaigns, so I had some bronzed inside out pants and whatnot. I had a bunch of boxes and I packed my stuff up, still stupefied at what had happened. I had never been fired before in my life. Not once. I knew that the Ahhh! folks would write me a decent letter of recommendation, because it was just too dangerous to write someone a bad rec and then get sued, but people would be able to connect the dots if they tried hard enough. I had been canned, and when word got around that the wonderboy of Trouble Jeans had gotten the boot, they would make up their own reasons. So it might get a little dicey finding work in Boston anytime soon. Relocation wouldn't normally be a difficulty, but there was Grandma. Unless I wanted to dump this whole thing on my parents and have to explain everything to them, I would have to stay close to Boston.

"You don't have to be right when you're white," Ruley had said, time and again. I always knew that this was more or less the truth, but I figured it really applied to the borderline negroes, not people like me. Face it: I was still a sucker for the American Dream. Upward mobility, the glide path to success as long as all your Ts were crossed, your Is were dotted, and your name wasn't Shaniqua or Fatrelle.

As I turned toward the door, there was Stewart, dressed in his security outfit and looking embarrassed.

"What're you doing on day shift?" I said.

He shrugged, started to say something, then caught himself and gave a little jerk of his head.

"You all set?"

I laughed. "No," I said, "actually I'm not. I don't have a job. And do you know what they call a Negro Without a Job?"

Stewart looked even more uncomfortable. He shook his head.

"Same thing they call a Negro who's a doctor," I said.

He gave me a blank look. "I don't get it."

"Yeah, well, maybe it'll come to you."

He followed me down the hall. I can honestly say, of the thousands of times I had walked down that hall the past two years, the only times I had seen it so empty had been when I had gotten there an hour and a half before opening to do some extra work. You would think the Vacuum of the Gods had sucked everybody out of the place. It must have been really crowded in the bathrooms.

Going down the escalator to the main lobby, I could feel the eyes of my former co-workers on my back. I suppressed the urge to give them all the finger.

"Well, hey, uh, man," Stewart said, opening the front door for me. "See you around, okay?"

"See me around?" I said. "Man, where are you going to see me? Huh? Do you even know where I live?"

His eyes narrowed then, and I couldn't tell if it was fear or anger behind them.

"Well, well okay, then," he said. And he turned and closed the door.

Grandma was in the Sun Room, propped up in a chair, her face shaded with a large straw hat. The sun sliced the room in half, gold light inching toward her.

"It's hot out here," she said.

"It *is* the Sun Room," I said.

"Still. They should put the air conditioning up." She pointed to a table just beyond her reach. A bottle of Deel!ght sat shaded by a parasol with a straw in it. "Can you fetch that for me?"

"I thought you didn't like it."

I got her the bottle.

"You make do," she said. She looked up at me. Squinted. "They fire you yet?"

"Last week."

She did some figuring.

"How come you haven't been out to see me then?"

"Been busy."

"Busy? You ain't got a job."

"Working with my lawyer. We worked out a severance package in exchange for not suing them."

She shook her head and sipped some flat cherry soda.

"If you had followed my advice, you'd be owning them instead of cashing their check."

"I guess I should have," I said. "But that's done now."

"Hmmm," she said. "Well, what you gonna do?"

I had thought of just lying low for a couple of months and checking out my options, take some trips. I had money in the bank, so bills weren't a problem. But I'm not the kind of guy to stay put, especially when I feel I've got something to prove, so I had decided instead to open my own marketing firm. We would specialize in consumer end users, multi-ethnic products. I had a rolodex full of contacts, folks I knew could get the job done.

"I'm going to open my own business," I said. "Be my own boss."

"Well," she said, "I got just two words of advice for you."

"Uh huh?"

"One, don't represent nobody that can't make a decent soda pop, and two, you gonna go into this, you go all the way. Got it?"

"Yes, ma'am."

The path of the sun had brought the laser beam of light perilously close to the armrest of her chair. She looked down at the sun, then up at me. I scooted her chair farther into the shade.

"What you gonna call your business? I hope it's not one of those African- or Muslim-sounding names: 'Muhammad Marketing.'"

"BTN Enterprises," I said.

She sipped from her straw, then started laughing and blew cherry soda out of her nose.

"Shame on you!" she said when she finally caught her breath.

When I left my grandmother in the sun room, I was, if not in good spirits, then certainly in a neutral mood. Things were out of whack, but they would be okay. Repaired. But when I left the nursing home, walking out into the parking lot to look for the Rover sent me back a week to the day I had been fired.

Out of force of habit I had walked to my usual parking space, forgetting the car that had been parked there. I was standing there, confused, staring at the Buick Park Avenue, when someone called out to me.

"Hey!"

I turned to see TONICA shuffling toward me, arthritic hips swinging wide like he was astride a fat horse.

"Hey, there, nigger!" he said.

"*What?*" I asked. "You talking to *me?*"

The words bubbled out of him as he stomped toward me. "You ain't carjacking *me*, nigger, oh no, not *today*! You common *thief*!"

I stood my ground and he got up in my face. I could smell the sour aroma of old man and mothballs. He held a gnarled, ashy finger under my nose. The corners of his mouth were daubed with foamy spittle. One punch, I knew, would do him, probably do him for good. He'd fall, break a hip, be laid up in a hospital for weeks, get pneumonia, die. Murder. I squeezed my cardboard box until my fingers hurt.

"Get out of my way, old man." I said.

He cringed as though I had coughed up phlegm into his face, then snatched his arm back and made a fist. For an instant I imagined that it was I who was going to go down to the pavement, break a hip, get laid up, die. Well, it would be a fitting end to the day. I braced for the blow.

But then his eyes widened, his face softened, and he lowered his hand.

"Do—do I know you?" he asked.

"What?"

"Do I know you?" he said again, his gravelly voice softening. He cocked his head from side to side, then held up a finger, smiling. "You from down Galveston way?"

"What?" I said. "No. What are you old, man—crazy?"

He leaned close and peered into my face, his eyes darting across my features. "No no no, let me see. No. Shreveport!" He laughed. "You one them Shreveport boys, ain't you? You a Jenkins, ain't you? You a Jenkins, I can see it in your eyes. How are your people, son? Why, I haven't seen one of your folks in Lord knows how long. We kin, you know!" He looked down at my box and it was as though he hadn't noticed it until now. He pulled his chin in, narrowed his eyes, then reached and gently put his big hands half on mine, half on the box.

"Son," he said, "Son, is it heavy?"

o**ff**icial **F**riend

The last time I saw Professor Klem, the late morning sun a crimson nimbus behind his famous head of glistening Gorgon hair, he was on his way to being murdered at Lucy MacIntosh's house by Lucy's husband, Leif. Leif was supposed to be away on business all weekend, but, in fact, suspecting that his wife was cheating on him, he had merely concocted an elaborate tale of urgent business in Toronto[1], certain that he could lure her into making a fatal mistake. At his trial, Leif said that he was sorry that he had shot Professor Klem because he thought he was an okay guy—"I mean, I liked his poems, even though they were love poems to my own wife; they made me laugh"—but he had just finished shooting Lucy and he knew he had to go through with it and make the whole thing complete, so he shot Professor Klem, too, though not as many times as he had shot Lucy. "It—it seemed like the thing to do," Leif said. The jury

---

[1]Rather than meeting with a minor official in the Toronto Sanitation Department to discuss a change in specifications on a flush valve control unit which his company was bidding on, he was waiting in his study with a pint of Southern Comfort to steel his nerves and a shiny new 9mm pistol he had bought at WalMart clutched in his hairy fist.

deliberated 65 minutes, convicted him and sentenced him to death. If he had not made the Toronto plans, the jury said later, they would have given him life. "But the fake Toronto plans mean premeditation, and premeditation means the death chamber," the jury foreman explained on TV after the trial. Leif is still appealing his sentence, though not the conviction. "I did it," he said, "but I don't want to die just yet. I don't want to have to face Lucy. She looked really pissed when I was shooting her."

When I last saw him, Professor Klem was waving and smiling as he crossed Lorraine Street on the way to the 14th Street bus stop, some chrysanthemums wrapped in blue paper in one hand, a fifth of gin in a paper bag in the other. He always traveled by bus or train, occasionally taxi, since he had never learned to drive and did not own a bicycle. I knew he was on his way to meet a woman—the flowers were a dead giveaway—but also because *that*, besides writing and translating poetry and teaching two classes per semester, is what he did. He wooed women. Pursued them. Was pursued by them. Entertained them. Romanced them. You think of a verb vis-a-vis women that resulted in Professor Klem "getting in they drawers," as one of my friends said, and he did it. "The woman?" he said to me once, shrugging, smiling that disarming smile. "I am for the woman always. It is like she is to me the air of breathing, the water to my soul." And so on. He was a poet after all.

I never met Lucy MacIntosh, never even knew she existed, although, of course, I knew of Professor Klem's sad and prodigious needs and so knew that there was always a woman at the end of his bus or taxi ride. He rarely entertained at his modest bungalow, preferring to be a guest in the homes of his lady friends. Perhaps this was part of a death wish The pictures they ran of Lucy MacIntosh in the newspaper didn't flatter her much. Washed out and fleshy with small eyes and a crooked mouth, she looked like a woman wanted by the police for mistreating dogs or passing bad checks at a tattoo parlor, not the critical, fatal, irresistible hinge in a deadly ménage à trois. For some reason they listed her height, which was 5'4", though, equally inexplicably, not her weight. You would think that the newspapers would try and find some decent pictures of a woman murdered by an enraged, heartbroken husband who caught her in the act (and I mean *really* in the act; during the trial the prosecution presented forensic evidence that proved that Lucy, who was astride Professor Klem, actually died while he was still inside her), to show how she was so irresistible that the poor schmuck who got killed with her couldn't resist her feminine wiles, and that the poor schmuck who killed her couldn't live without her. Apparently not, though. Maybe the newspapers wanted to show her as a not particularly attractive housewife drudge so they could play up the "mystery of love" angle. You know: you see a couple in public and you wonder, what does she/he see in him/her? That mystery probably kept thousands of people scratching their heads as they read about the trial every day or watched the live feed from the courtroom on the public access channel. Maybe it also made people wonder about how sexed up Lucy must have been, how maybe she made up for her lack of looks by being a real freak in the sack. I know it certainly intrigued me. I tried to look into those beady little eyes and imagine her staring in a sultry fashion at Professor Klem, luring him into her fatal embrace. She must have had tricks up her sleeve, and her skirt, that mesmerized him, tantalized him, compromised him. Otherwise it just didn't make any sense.

Professor Klem was a handsome man, which further deepens and complicates the whole Lucy MacIntosh angle. Not tall, maybe ten pounds overweight, he was olive-complected, had a jaw line that looked like it had been chiseled by Michelangelo, and a head of glistening black unruly hair that coiled, Medusa-like, over a brooding brow that shadowed penetrating cobalt blue eyes which people *swore* were contacts. Poetry, romance, suffering: he had it all, and all that he had, women wanted in the worst way. I actually witnessed women quivering in his presence.

Professor Klem was a political refugee who washed up on the shores of Southern State U. from his homeland, Urbithia, a semi-autonomous region in the former Soviet Republic of Moldavia. A lifelong patriot for Urbithian self-determination, he had been fired from his lectureship at the State University of Moldavia for his agitation for full statehood for his homeland and had had his books removed from libraries and bookstores and burned in public ("Murder My Babies," his poem about this event, is often anthologized in collections of political protest poems). Then he had then suffered tortures at the hands of the state police that he would still not talk about ten years after the fact, but the lingering effects of which you could always read in his soulful eyes. He was an avid, though inept, basketball player, lingering on the court for hours in Mendermen Gym playing pick-up games with other faculty and students, working up a tremendous sweat and confusing people on both teams with his shouted encouragements and directions in Urbithian. He would leave the court dripping wet, but no one ever saw him in the showers. The standard theory was that, as a Stinky European—and we had all had experiences with European students and visiting faculty members, and they seemed to come in one variety, Stinky—he showered just once a week. The alternative theory, and one which picked up credence over time, was that he was sensitive about his torture wounds, because when his team was asked to go "skins" on the court, he would politely demure and, if pressed, would leave the court and await another game. Eventually people would stop demanding that he "skin up," the result being that members of the other team would mistakenly toss him the ball half a dozen times during the game, often titling the outcome of the contest. Bad things had been done to him by the State Police of Urbithia at the behest of their Moldavian masters, we surmised, and he wanted to spare onlookers from the reminders of his suffering. During the course of Leif MacIntosh's trial, however, when the prosecution displayed autopsy photos of the dead poet, the only blemishes on his pale torso were the two surprisingly small wounds in his chest made by Leif's 9mm Wal-Mart pistol.

I was Professor Klem's official friend. When he had arrived from Urbithia ten years ago, by way of short stays in New York City and Abilene, Kansas, to begin his tenure as Associate Professor of Eastern European Literature, someone in the administration (prompted by concerns for what a funny-talking foreigner with a reputation for sexual hijinks—his reputation had preceded him—might run into in a small southern town), decided that he needed looking after. So he was assigned an official friend, usually a graduate student who could use the extra money and didn't have the distractions and time constraints that undergrads and other professors had. I was the fifth of the official friends, and my tenure as such was the shortest-lived, for I lasted only eight months before Professor Klem was killed. When he died I felt sad that he was dead, guilty that I couldn't stop him from getting killed, and, yes, anxious about money. I was getting $400 a month to look out for him.

Professor Klem never knew he had official friends. Had he known, he would have been profoundly insulted, as would any of his self-respecting countrymen. An Urbithian expert in Washington with the State Department (he had actually known Professor Klem when he had been assigned to the American embassy in Chisinau) had advised the university NOT to assign Professor Klem an official friend and then, failing to short circuit this policy, had warned the administration that it would be disastrous if he ever found out about the official friends. How disastrous? someone in the administration had asked. *Utterly* disastrous, the expert had warned. But if he *had* found out about us, though he would have been offended, he wouldn't have *done* anything about it. That was another thing about Urbithian honor: it didn't allow confrontating or embarrassing someone else. He would have suffered in silence.

I got the job because a buddy of mine, Clay Steckler, had

completed his PhD in Physics the year before and was working in the Dean of the Faculty's office while he looked for "the right position." He came up to me one day in the Anthropology Department's graduate lounge and put an envelope in my hand.

"What's this?" I asked.

"It's a job application."

"I already have a job."

"This one's a good job. Trust me."

I was one of several TA's for the two sections of the Anthropology Department's most popular undergraduate course—Caucasians and Cannibals—which meant that I had to read about two hundred uninspired journal entries from marginally literate undergraduates twice a week and lead highly frustrating discussions with truculent attendants about cultural differences on Thursday evenings.

"I don't have time for another job," I said, not believing the words coming out of my own mouth. "I'm TA-ing two classes and getting my dissertation committee together."

"$400 *a month*," Clay said, his voice a sing-song children's taunt.

"*Four* hundred?"

Clay nodded.

"Four hundred?" I said again.

Now, to you in the real world, $400 a month might seem like chicken feed, but to a doctoral student in his sixth year of graduate school teaching two classes for $600 a month and barely keeping afloat, nearly doubling your income is serious money. I opened the envelope and read the application.

"It doesn't say what I'd be doing," I said.

"It's simple. You'll be somebody's friend."

I looked at him.

"What?"

Clay sat down on the sofa next to me.

"You know Professor Klem?" he said.

"The poet guy? Plays ball in Menderman? The weird one?"

I was already thinking about the $400 a month with one part of my brain. An i-Pod just blooped into my head like a piece of popcorn bursting in slow motion. *Blooooop.*

"They like to call him eccentric. He's brilliant in his field."

"Yeah, what's that?"

"Translating Urbithian literature. I've never read any of it, but they say he's the best in the world. The thing is, though, he—he just doesn't make friends that well because, well, he's just eccentric, you know?"

"So the University hires him a friend?"

"More or less. It's just a way of keeping track of him so he doesn't get hurt or anything. Doesn't, you know, insult people or wind up in jail. We've got the best Urbithian literary scholar in the world and we've got to protect that."

"Or else what?"

Clay shrugged. "I don't know. I never asked. I just, you know, hang out with Professor K, give him a ride when he needs it, double date."

"Double date?" I said. The term raised unsettling prospects for me. I hadn't had much success with women recently. I'm a fairly average-looking guy, no Brad Pitt, but I'm devoid of scars, unsightly bumps and general disfigurement, so I *could*, if I needed to, get a date now and then, but in those days I had a lot on my mind. I didn't have the time to pursue the whole dating thing. Would I be expected to come up with dates on the spur of the moment so I could accompany Professor Klem? My i-Pod (I was already creating playlists) evaporated.

"Don't worry," Clay said. "His lady friends almost always have friends to tag along. They may be a little older than us, but, you know . . . ." He winked at me, I raised my eyebrow, and he nodded, smirking.

I looked at the application, which Clay had already filled out for me. His printing was much neater than mine. I guess all those lab reports made him concentrate on his penmanship.

"Is this like a spy thing or something? Do I have to, like, fill out forms and shit? Report back on what he does, keep a log book or something?" I leaned closer and whispered. "Is he under surveillance?"

Clay shrugged.

"I don't know about the surveillance thing, man. Hey, Patriot Act, anything's possible. But no one ever asked me to fill out a report or anything like that. I just kept him out of trouble."

"How'd you do that?" I asked. I envisioned Clay breaking up a bar fight between Professor Klem and a tattooed biker with teeth sharpened to points and a steel plate in his head.

"Don't let him drink too much, make sure he doesn't insult people."

This was in the ballpark of what I had suspected.

"He insults people? Like, regularly?"

"It's a language thing. People take him the wrong way sometimes. What might work in a poem sometimes doesn't go over well down at Lenny's."

Lenny's was a local watering hole notorious for the townie fights students would get into.

"I don't know," I said.

"And I got a nice unofficial check every month."

"Unofficial?"

"As in, no withholding," he said. He made a little sliding motion with his hand, something—an envelope—being slipped somewhere—under a door?—and smiled. "You know. Unofficial checks for the official friend."

"$400," I said.

"Just sign the application and turn it in. Like I said, the job's already yours. I gave you an excellent recommendation."

"Thanks?" I said.

Literary translators are like the second cousins once removed (with warts) of writers and poets. Unsung, unknown, unappreciated, few of them ever achieve fame, and if they do it is fame lite, recognition among other translators, among scholars, among the foreign writers who need translators. Nobody in the real world knows who they are. But Professor Klem defied the odds and achieved fame in just that fashion—as a translator—most probably because the best poems he translated were his own. His fame transcended the usual boundaries. People outside of the "translation ghetto," as I once heard it described, knew his name. Hollywood types knew him because of his personal story of triumph over oppression and overwhelming odds. (Hollywood loves stories of triumph over oppression and overwhelming odds.) *Time* once included him in their yearly "40 To Watch Under 40" piece: "With smoldering good looks that alone could have melted the ice of the Cold War, eyes that betray a wounded, fragile, but stalwart soul, and a knack for striking images and unexpected metrical dynamics, this dreamy Moldavian poet has set the literary world abuzz with his third book, 'My Juicy Ice.'" His poems were cool enough that several had been turned into rock songs by groups like the Polish grunge wannabe band Crosshatch Testing and the American boy band Hip Flexor. His most famous work, however, remained only a poem:

> I was in the courtyard watching the ice falling
> Watching the falling ice, the melting ice
> like broken airplanes, like broken airplanes
> With wings of brittle translucence.
> Your heart, you said, demands a jealous heart,
> Like the ocean demands the fleshy mouths of rivers
> full of melting ice to fill its secret places.
> The wonderment of life overcomes you. Bleed.
> Why have you sought my lips? My eyes?

Is my heart large enough for your desire?
Is it I who has traveled over mountains
jagged, terrible, indifferent to suffering? Or perhaps
you have noticed the injustice of love
And stood trembling in the rain, offering
my own skin as recompense?

I'm an anthropologist, not an artist or a literary scholar, so I don't know if it's that good of a poem. It confuses me, I confess. But google "Professor Klem" and about three times more than not, this poem is what you'll find, and then, on blogs and message boards, breathless prose from (usually) women attesting to how moving and "complete" it is, and how, for some of them, it changed their lives.

Professor Klem's penis was 3 3/4" long, fully erect. I found a picture of it, measured against a ruler, on his computer in a folder named "Evidence" after I was sent to his apartment to box up his belongings following the murder. It was a disquieting business, going through his things. For one thing, the man's smell was everywhere. He had one of those heavy musky body aromas that penetrate fabric and linger long after the fact. Each room was pungent with his goaty afterfunk. And because the place smelled so strongly of him, I expected at any moment that I would turn a corner and there he would be, sitting at his desk, glasses perched on his nose, one hand running through his glorious hair while the other held pen poised above notebook, and he would be saying, "searching for the American." Of course, that didn't happen, but being there did settle one thing for me: if the university had been using me as a spy, they certainly wouldn't have sent me over on my own to box up his stuff.

So I wasn't a spy, but I wasn't much of an estate executor either, which the university kind of foisted on me. They had all manner of agreements in place to use his manuscripts, house his papers, reprint his poems, but the sofas and the extra hand towels and the bric-a-brac?

We had no record of any family to whom to send his personal effects and possessions, so that's why I looked on the computer. Professor Klem's C drive was the repository of a lot of strange stuff—political propaganda about things that had happened to the Urbithians in World War II at the hands of the Moldavians and the Russians and the Germans and the Rumanians; a collection of jpegs of Betty Boop memorabilia; a ton of first-person shoot-'em-up computer games like SplatterFest and My Bullet, Your Brain; webcam video captures from locations around the world at twilight—but concerning things of a sexual nature, I would have to say that the penis pic was the strangest. And there were no addresses, e-mail or physical, of any kind. I thought I would find the Moldavian address of a cousin, or the Chicago address of a great-uncle. Nothing. The man had become completely uprooted from his past. It was as though he had sprouted out of the earth, fully grown.

Professor Klem's penis was smaller than mine. By how much I won't say. Let it suffice, though, that I was encouraged when I saw the photo. If he got lucky with *that*, then there certainly was hope for me. Of course, there's the whole suffering-poet angle, too, but I would think that if size really did matter, it wouldn't make a difference *how* romantic and *poetic* you were if, once it came time to get down to business, you pulled out less than half a ballpark frank. Some have said that the penis couldn't have been his own. Who would record their own substandard equipment? Well, I don't know the reason for the photo, but I do know that it was his, because I have slept with a few women who had been lovers of his and they have confirmed his below average size. Despite this, they all maintained, to a woman, that he was a wonderful, considerate, inventive, and surprisingly energetic lover, capable of great endurance. "He would just kind of go away behind his eyes, like he had this secret place," one woman said, she herself getting a far away look as she spoke, "and then he'd make love to me for *hours*."

I imagined that he was utilizing a technique he had perfected during his stints in State Police custody for his "subversive activities" back in his homeland. One of the Urbithian State Police's favorite interrogation techniques was to stick electric cattle prods up prisoners' rectums. (Professor Klem never admitted to this kind of abuse to me or any of his other official friends, or even to his lovers, as far as I can tell, but I have it on good authority from a friend in Denver that an ex-Urbithian State Policeman who, ironically enough, also writes poetry, some of it detailing his interrogations back in the homeland, has identified this particular technique as wonderfully effective on 'malcontents and subversives, but especially poets.') The cattle prods came out and Professor Klem disengaged himself from himself, astral projected, went away, endured stoically. Later, when he could put to use under much better circumstances what he had learned in Cell Block Z,[2] he would engage his own personal autopilot, prolong his sexual performance, and endear himself to scores of women.

I studied up on Professor Klem before I made my move to become his friend. Clay gave me a full rundown on Professor Klem—favorite foods: barbecued ribs and Urbithian parsnip pie; favorite sport: ice hockey; favorite type of movie: American action adventure; favorite time of day: dawn; etc.—and I watched him from afar for a week or so, taking notes. I read the three volumes of his poetry that he had so far translated into English and found his work to indeed be, as one of the dust cover blurbs read, "evocative, quirky, disturbing and wacky." If I had had the time, I would have tried to use my secret status as his official friend to get into one of his

[2]*Cell Block Z* became the title of the definitive biography of Professor Klem. His biographer, Mireille Sloane, maintains that Klem's entire adult identity was both erased and reformed in Cell Block Z, and that, in an ironic twist, he owed his lasting literary fame to the astounding creativity provoked by his equally creative torturers in prison.

classes, which were notoriously over-enrolled. He not only did a class on the poetry of former Soviet Republics, Urbithia included, but a class on Moldavian folk art as well, focusing on traditional ballads and *Straphsha*, the ritualized Urbithian insult genre made popular in the west by Billy Crystal in his movie, *East Meets West.* The classes were usually overwhelmingly female, a 5:1 ratio. Word was, whichever of his coeds Professor Klem didn't choose, guys in the classes, provided they weren't gag ugly, could have their pick. People called it "the halo effect."

But I figured the best way to befriend Professor Klem was to start playing basketball. I had been on my high school team (I was one of those guys who got to play the last minute and a half of blowout games) and I still had some moderate skills, so I started hanging out at the courts and playing with Professor Klem when I got the chance. He wasn't very good—dribbled the ball like he was hammering nails and never looked up until it was too late to make a pass or see a defender descending upon him; had a two-handed girly set shot; threw passes soccer style, two handed over his head—but he played very tenacious defense, which meant, basically, that he mauled people. And most of the guys playing were students who didn't want to look like they were crybabies, so they let him get away with a lot. The first game I got into with him, I was on the opposite team, and as luck would have it, we were guarding each other. Halfway through the game, during which we had held each other scoreless, I got the ball in the low post and turned for a shot. He grunted something in Urbithian and swatted at the ball, missing it completely and poking me in the eye instead. I went down in a heap and he stood there, so I was told, with his hands on his head as though he thought his scalp was going to float away. "So sorry, my friend, so sorry," he kept saying. He escorted me to the student health center, waited with me for two hours until a doctor could see me and announce that I had gotten "the snot smacked out of my cornea" and prescribe me an eye patch and some drops, then rode a

Kurt Jose Ayau

university bus with me home. "So sorry, my friend," he kept saying. And after that, we were, indeed, friends.

I would see Professor Klem several times a week. We'd play hoops, have a coffee together some mornings, do a movie. He took an interest in my dissertation, the effects of the Internet on dating and marriage patterns in Appalachia (The University of Southern Georgia Press has offered a contract; tentative title, *The End of Incest: The Internet and Appalachian Mating Practices*) and offered his insights on the web. "It is like life growing from a single cell, yes? We just do not know what kind of life it is yet. Perhaps it is a cancer?" I had never thought of it that way, but I had to admit that he might have a point.

Once we double dated at an Urbithian folk festival he organized. His date was a stunning Bulgarian woman, a visiting Slavic languages scholar on loan to us for a semester from Columbia, mine a student of hers who had a large mole not quite dead center on her forehead. The moment I met Sasha, I couldn't keep the word "Cyclopia" from resonating in my mind. I felt particularly put off by the fact that she was an American, third generation, not Eastern European. A mole on an Eastern European woman is exotic; on an American girl, you're just wondering, "Why don't you get that thing burned off with some liquid nitrogen?" She was nice, though. We ended up hooking up that night and saw each other off and on for a few months. In fact, I was with her when I heard the news about Professor Klem.

Professor Klem's women were numerous, and they all, with the exception of Lucy McIntosh, were beautiful, cosmopolitan, intelligent, accomplished, urbane. Which made the fact of Lucy McIntosh that much more perplexing, a mystery of the highest order. One interpretation of the Lucy MacIntosh perplexity could be a recitation of the familiar claptrap about the strangeness of love. I believe that he could have loved many of the women he dated, that he could even have chosen any one of them as a long-term lover or wife. After all, life partners are people with whom you share, or could share, hopes and dreams, people with whose minds you have found a simpatico connection. Soulmates. A long-term relationship, one that really warrants the term, cannot be built simply upon sex. This is why, I think, Leif McIntosh made a great mistake in killing both his wife and Professor Klem. He was not going to lose his wife to the great Urbithian romantic. The affair would have passed, one (most certainly Professor Klem) tiring of the other (undoubtedly Lucy McIntosh). But Leif, judging from his self-incriminating testimony, was not the kind of guy who spent much time working such things out. His responses were immediate, territorial, irreversible. His property was being infringed, and so he would put a permanent end to the infringement. Obviously, however, he infringed upon himself by denying himself of Lucy forever after. But, again, Leif didn't seem to be a guy who thought that far ahead, his Toronto ruse notwithstanding.

Professor Klem's funeral was enormous, the kind of event normally associated with lifelong residents whose abiding civic virtues and passions for giving embed themselves into a town's psyche; for politicians or celebrities; for patriarchs or matriarchs of multi-generational dynasties. Professor Klem, of course, was none of these things. He was a funny-talking, usually malodorous Eastern European who translated obscure poetry for the state college press and who fucked a whole lot of local women. This is not to diminish his achievement, however. Screwing lots of women is a demanding task.

It was, as funerals go, an interesting affair. Since Professor Klem's reputation as a love machine was widespread, I suspected that many of the "mourners" at his funeral were merely curious, hoping to identify his former lovers among the others crowding the funeral home. People were trying to connect the dots. Six degrees of Klem's dick. Most folks didn't know who most of those former lovers *were*, so I think there was much wild speculating going on, countless little exchanges, conversations, queries. And that lead to people leaving with folks with whom they hadn't arrived. I myself (one of three eulogists) arrived alone and left with Marcia Carson, a 5'10" forever-legged real estate agent who had sold Professor Klem his home, then ridden his 3 3/4" love stump for several months before the inevitable pained, tearful goodbye.

"You were his friend," she said to me in her Lexus on the way from the funeral home where his ashes had reposed in a traditional Urbithian clay pot.

"Yes."

"A friend of the male variety. That's rare."

"I suppose."

I've never been that skillful in repartee with women, certainly not gorgeous women like Marcia Carson, who, I'm sure, sold more than a few houses just on her looks. Looking at her made me wonder why Professor Klem would ever dump her. How could you go from Marcia Carson to Lucy McIntosh? It hadn't been a straight line from Marcia to Lucy, but from what I saw at the funeral, *any* of those women outdid Lucy MacIntosh. When you're capable of Marcia, why even think about Lucy?

"I counted eighteen women there I know he slept with," she said, shaking her magnificently styled hair. It was auburn colored and shoulder length. I could smell her shampoo, something fruity. "Who knows how many were there I didn't know." She angrily lit a cigarette. "It's a wonder half the town didn't come down with something. The man couldn't keep it in his pants."

I was about to make a joke and say how relatively easy that should have been, given its size, but realized that she was all too aware of Professor Klem's shortcomings in that regard.

She started to make a funny sound that I realized was crying, then almost as quickly stopped. She drew deeply on her cigarette and blew the smoke out the moon roof.

"Where do you live?" she asked.

I gave her my address, a graduate student housing apartment. She shook her head.

"I can't have sex there," she said. "Too many people would see me."

I almost said, "What?" out loud, but I kept my mouth shut long enough for the moment to pass. A few seconds later I said, "Your place would be fine."

Marcia Carson made me take a shower, then got me high on criminally potent weed, lead me to her bed and nearly turned me inside out. When we were done I thanked her.

"Don't thank me," she said, shrugging her bra on. "Thank Leif MacIntosh."

And a funny thing happened after that. Word must have gotten around. Marcia, being in a "people business," making all those contacts, must have mentioned my friendship with Professor Klem and the afternoon she had had with me, because suddenly women, the Professor's former lovers, started, well, there's no better way of putting it than just to say they started falling out of the sky. I'd be in the grocery store and a woman would appear next to me in the frozen vegetable section and say, "Oh, weren't you at Professor Klem's funeral? Aren't you his friend?" And soon enough, away to the races we'd go. I'd say that after Professor Klem died, I lost about six months of work on my dissertation, but all and all, it was time pretty well spent.

The women were young and not-so-young, white, Asian, African-American, Eurotrash. There were three doctors, a lawyer, an engineer, a daycare supervisor, a Methodist minister, two aerobics instructors, coeds, an associate dean, a couple of waitresses, an airline pilot. We had sex in cars, *on* cars, in a cemetery, in a church, in the sparsely occupied balcony of the Revival House Art Theatre, in tubs (full and empty), on tables, under tables, in closets, in a small plane, on boats, in an administrative office. It was like they were trying one last time to connect with Professor Klem, like I had a Ouija dick or something, because they never, not one of them, ever called me again. They'd screw me, thank me, and leave. And I'd thank Leif MacIntosh.

The University informed me that I could continue earning my $400 per month by, in effect, managing Professor Klem's estate. I had no experience in such matters, but if they were willing to continue paying me, I wasn't going to argue with them. I guess they figured it was a whole lot cheaper than hiring a lawyer. So I would go over once a week and organize things for the auction that would conclude the late professor's relationship with Southern State and America. (His ashes had already been taken back to Urbithia by a fellow expatriate poet living in Milwaukee.)[3] We were going to sell everything he had, including the house, for which he had paid cash, and donate the proceeds to his favorite charity, The Children of Urbithia.

Cleaning out the house, I found some old family photos, archaic with their scalloped white borders, faded documentation of dreary everyday life in the Soviet Union. The Klem family—father Stroidgin, Mother Liipschka, sisters Maimele and Gripsjanja, brothers Lupreclil, Yarno and Zlalek, and, of course, the professor—posed amidst large (but nonetheless depressing-looking) meals, rode bicycles, played chess. All of the pictures were taken around the same time because no one in the Klem family aged. Throughout the photos, Professor Klem brooded, glared, stared soulfully into the camera, the future poet a chrysalis visible behind the stiffly crossed arms, the cocked head, the stormy eyes. Every one else in his family

[3]Poetry, apparently, is to Urbithia what soccer is to every other country on the other side of the Atlantic. "Without poetry," an old Urbithian saying goes, "life is dry goat cheese."

seemed light-hearted and carefree, even though they were living in the Soviet Union. It was as though young Sczhlame Uderbarz absorbed the family's pain.

I also found some home-made CDs of the Klatcha Sisters, Urbithian Folk Singers whose tremulous vocal arrangements, discovered by a Hollywood producer while on location in nearby Rumania, have been featured in several recent art films. (The CDs pre-date their Hollywood work and are much better, if you ask me.) The CDs were packaged in those thin jewel cases for homemade CDs whose spindles always get crushed, the cover art simple photographs of the sisters, signed and dated on the back. I can't read Urbithian, but something about the handwriting on those messages, the gentle, looping, sinuous curves of the penmanship, suggests intimate relationships. Gertha and Yathnamia, the twins, are fairly attractive, but Miliezcthe, the youngest sister, the dirty blonde, is absolutely stunning. I yearned for her and envied Professor Klem. But not for long, since, after all, he was dead.

And I found poems, hundreds of them. Most were in Urbithian, hence meaningless to me, but here and there I found some in English, although nearly all of them were in the stanza style of classic Urbithian *stragas,* which have an aaaaaab bbbbbbc cccccccd rhyme scheme and are, predictably, quite tedious. I also found several poems that were addressed to "My Friends." One, I felt, seemed like it might have been written to me. It wasn't very long.

> The eye tells of the friend's loyalty.
> It bleeds for pain of the friend.
> It cries for love of the friend.
> It is the avenue of the soul of the friend.
> The eye.
> It is an orb, yes.
> It is of many facets, yes.
> It is of pulsing singularities, yes.

It is the avenue of the soul of the friend.
The eye. The friend. They are one.

And there were photographs of Professor Klem's lovers, color computer printouts from digital cameras. Why he didn't simply save the photos on his computer, rather than print them all, I don't know, some kind of Old World nostalgia, distrust of the computer, what have you. But there was a stack of them. 43 women, all naked, except for one, and all posed like old-time Playboy Playmates—alluring, sexy, yet tastefully comported. Marcia Carson was stunning in stiletto heels and a corset, holding a kitten. Seeing among these photographs pictures of women I had slept with, I was newly grateful for their kindness, newly aroused at seeing what, in some cases, I had only groped feverishly in darkened cars, licked briefly through the narrowest of gaps between shirt buttons, and chagrined that none of them found me worthy of so much as a follow-up call or a postcard after our frenzied hookups.

How trusting of them to do this for him. I flipped through the pictures again and again, wondering at their—their what? Gullibility? Naiveté? Submission? In this day of ubiquitous internet porn, who can be assured that their naked bodies won't show up on some website or posted to some discussion group? But the one who wasn't naked. I came back to her once I had satisfied myself, looking at the others, that I had identified all the women I had screwed in behalf of Professor Klemp.

It was Lucy MacIntosh. She sat primly in a pink jumpsuit on a straight-backed chair, staring directly into the camera, unsmiling, her legs together, her hands on her knees. I remembered then what Professor Klem had said to me the last time I had seen him.

He was carrying chrysanthemums and a fifth of gin. He was smiling.

"Come with me, my friend," he said. "And we will make some good fun!"

I didn't understand then, but now it is clear: he was suggesting a three-way with Lucy MacIntosh that afternoon. Now *that* certainly would have put Leif over the edge. If being betrayed by your wife with one man could drive you to murder, what could finding her with *two* men do to you?

I asked a friend about this, an Abnormal Psych student working on her dissertation. (I was too embarrassed to ask any of the faculty.) She told me to give her a few days to think about it and consult a few journals.

When she called me at home several days later I had almost forgotten that I had asked her for something.

"Dead," she said. "All of you."

"Dead? What?"

"You and Professor Klem and the woman and the husband, too."

"Really? All of us?"

"Especially you."

I thought about this for a second.

"How can you be especially dead?"

"Well, the husband knew about Klem. That's why he made the plans. But he wasn't figuring on you. The premeditated nature of the crime shows that he had moved beyond anger and was seeking revenge. Seeing you double-teaming his wife would have pushed him over the edge. He would have been *really* mad at you."

"Gee," I said. I found myself feeling hollowed out and suddenly cold. "Mad, huh?"

"We're talking torture mad. Blow off your testicles, chain you to a wall, let-the-rats-eat-you-and-watch-you-suffer mad. That kind of stuff."

I found it hard to swallow. I could barely croak out a thank you.

"You're welcome," she said. "Can I ask you something?"

"Sure."

"Had Professor Klem ever invited you to a threesome before?"

I was caught off guard by the question, my mind still trying to grapple with my brush with mortality.

"What?"

"Did he ever ask you to go on a date with him when it would just be you and him and one of his lady friends?"

"No. Not that I can remember."

"Interesting," she said, and then there was a long pause. "Well, okay. Thanks."

And she hung up.

I didn't want to believe her. I was Professor Klem's friend. Yes, an official friend at first, but we had grown close. It hadn't even bothered me how he smelled anymore.

Two weeks later I was boxing up the last of Professor Klem's belongings and a random sheet of paper slipped out of a three-ring binder that he had used to take notes for his translations. The sheet was a confusion of numbers, symbols and doodles, but in the center there were names. Five of them. Robey McManus, Daniel Showalter, Micky Grenz, Clay Steckler, and mine. Beside mine there was a small drawing. I later learned that it was a *Stropshkoviniepzcka*, the Urbithian symbol for bad luck and death.

But I didn't really need to know that, because the fact that he had written all our names down told me that he knew about us all, and that because he knew, that he was offended. True to the code of Urbithian honor, he had never said anything to us, but I guess he had finally had enough and so was going to solve the problem the only way, I guess, that seemed fitting to him. Suicide by Leif MacIntosh and, as an added bonus, a painful death for me.

That night, as I lay in bed trying to sleep, I kept replaying in my mind the last time I had seen him. The chrysanthemums. The fifth of gin. The steady stream of traffic on Lorraine Street that he had negotiated to get to the bus stop. And his eyes, his brilliant blue eyes, looking not at me, I now realized, but through me, to some other, farther, place.

Murray and the Holy Ghost

Tonight before he goes to sleep, as he has done every night for the past three weeks, Murray gets on his knees to check under the bed for the Holy Ghost.

"There's nothing under your bed," his mother says.

"I know that," Murray says, letting the bedspread fall back in place and climbing up on the bed. He pulls his Rocket Squid cartoon bedspread up to his chin and blinks at his mother. "Read me that story about Bloody Bones the Pirate again."

"Isn't that going to give you bad dreams?" his mother asks.

Murray shakes his head. "I don't dream about pirates."

His mother pulls the book from Murray's bookshelf and sits in the rocker next to the bed. She opens the book.

"'Yo ho ho and a bucket of blood,' yelled First Mate Billy Scars."

Murray lies in bed, the covers up to his nose now, and stares at the ceiling as his mother reads the tale of the infamous pirate, Bloody Bones. Murray's eyes, focused on the middle distance of nowhere, soon fill with images of the bobbing ship, *The Cutthroat*, its bright white sails puffing with wind, and the dastardly crew of murderers, thieves and scoundrels getting ready to attack an innocent cargo ship.

"The battle cry of the notorious pirate, Bloody Bones, filled the sails of his fearsome ship, *The Cutthroat*," his mother continues. "'Prepare for action!' First Mate Billy Scars cried."

Murray is almost immediately asleep, running a pirate movie in his mind, except the imagined sight of sails snapping in the wind reminds him of ghosts and thinking of ghosts gets him thinking of the Big Ghost, the Holy Ghost, and he shivers a little, but that soon passes and before his mother has reached page three, he is softly wheezing bubblegum toothpaste breath into his covers.

"Night, baby," his mother says and creeps from the room.

Recess. Grades one through three of Elmerville Elementary School are careering around the playground from monkey bars to four-square to tetherball to insect-smashing to kickball and back again like the frenzied electrons of an unstable atom. It is the first week in April and exuberant white clouds scud across the sky, dragging swift shadows over grass and asphalt and sand and metal.

Murray stands fifteen feet away from three of his friends who are using marbles to crush ants into the blacktop near the basketball court. The boys work silently while Murray shields his eyes from the sun with his hand and watches the clouds. Down here on the ground it is calm, but up there a fierce wind must be blowing, because the parade of clouds doesn't slow down. Murray tries to see shapes in the puffs and billows. Nothing. Nothing. Nothing. A poodle, maybe. Nothing. Nothing. A rocketship. Nothing. Nothing. A football.

A boy walks up to him and stands watching the sky.

"That big one there looks like boogers. That one there looks like boogers on a bicycle. That one there looks like a butt. That one looks like dinosaur poop."

Murray looks at the boy, who is picking his nose as he surveys the sky.

"What's dinosaur poop look like?" Murray asks.

The boy snorts. "Like that right there," he says, pointing to the cloud he has just described.

The boy is in one of the other second grade classes. Murray knows him only from chance encounters on the playground and the occasional inter-class kickball game. The word is that the kid eats boogers.

"A dinosaur butt," the kid says. "Dinosaur boogers."

Murray looks at the sky and out of the corner of his eye sees the kid slip his finger from his nose into his mouth. A booger eater.

Murray squints at the clouds. None of them comes close to looking like what Murray expects the Holy Ghost to look like. His expectations are vague, but he knows he'll know when he sees the right shape.

"A poodle with a shotgun," the kid next to him says. "Poodle boogers."

Sometimes Murray and his family go to church. Sometimes they don't. Today they do. It is a late Spring day, warm but not unpleasant, and the four of them ride in air conditioned silence to the shiny glass and brick building with the huge cross at the tip of its so-high roof. Murray knows that the cross means something, but it keeps getting mixed up in his mind with the flag and Abraham Lincoln. He knows that God is there in church and that it's a lot like school, with one person doing most of the talking and everybody else listening, but he doesn't mind that much because he likes school and the big open space above them in church makes him feel comfortable.

He follows his big sister and his parents into church, idly thinking about dinosaurs and robots. Inside everyone is smiling and cooing. He smells perfume and spearmint gum and cigarettes and aftershave. He follows his family into the big space and sits down between his big sister and his mother, so they can keep an eye on him. A lady comes by and hands his father a little bag of books and crayons and his father hands it to his mother and his mother hands it to him. There's a *Ranger Rick* magazine in the bag, a threadbare finger puppet, some candy wrappers, a coloring book, some crayons, most of them with their paper wrappers torn off, all of them broken and blunt. Organ music plays and the soft murmur of voices buzzes around him like a bag of bees. He flips through the coloring book looking for a fresh page as the music ends and the buzzing slowly dies down and Pastor Jim starts the first prayer.

Murray floats in and out of the prayers and the hymns, though he stands and sits on cue with everyone else. He thinks of an anthill he found behind the house yesterday and the way the ants were boiling all over each other and how they scared and fascinated him at the same time. He wanted to watch the ants and he wanted to destroy them. He wanted to save the world. He stomped the ants with his sneakers and then got water from the spigot and poured it on them, then got some dish soap from the kitchen and covered the ants and watched as the soapy goop slowly twitched and slid off the anthill. Then it was time to go in and watch tv. When he came out that afternoon, there was some goop still on the anthill and some curled up dead ants, but the live ants were gone.

Pastor Jim is reading the announcements and prayer concerns. Murray is intent on coloring a cowboy's hair green and purple, the broken crayons smudging over and beyond the lines like a kindergartner's coloring. Murray snorts in frustration and looks through the bag again. Maybe there's an unbroken crayon somewhere in the bottom that he missed. He scrapes the seam of the bag and finds only lint and scraps of paper.

It's time for the children's sermon, but Murray stays in his seat. The children's sermon is for preschool kids. Even though he really doesn't know what's going on, and his parents never bring him enough for him to be in Sunday School, Murray stays with the adults.

After the children's sermon, there's another hymn, then the

collection is taken up, with more singing, then it's time for the sermon.

Pastor Jim's voice washes over him like a warm wave, like honey being poured over a biscuit. Murray doesn't pay much attention because he can't. The words sail over his head, fly balls he can't catch. He looks at his cowboy's smudged purple and green hair, then thumbs through *Ranger Rick* again, thrilled by the pictures of snakes eating rodents. He looks at the stained glass windows. Murray doesn't hear Pastor Jim talking about the Holy Spirit, doesn't hear the warmth in Pastor Jim's voice as he talks about the Comforter and the Enabler. If the word *Ghost* were used, then Murray's ears would prick up, but in this church they don't use that word, but the word Spirit. Murray swings his feet and watches his scuffed shoes appear and disappear under the pew, appear and disappear, thinking of ants and dinosaurs and robots, floating on Pastor Jim's voice.

Dinnertime. Murray and Jennifer have been playing in the small plastic pool in the backyard, filling the water with toys, dirt, grass, squashed bugs. Jennifer is nine and should know better, as their mother always says, but an empty pool is no fun. Their mother calls them in and they reluctantly climb out, toes and fingers prune-wrinkly, grass sticking to their glistening skin. Their towels are hanging over the deck railing, but they run past them to the family room door, to be met by Mom, angry, who warns them if they value their hides they better towel off before coming in.

Chastised, they skulk back to the railing. Murray feels a shiver. He hadn't meant to make his mother angry. He grabs his towel and rubs himself so hard that his skin hurts. Jennifer gives herself a cursory toweling and into the house they go. Murray looks at the clock. 6:20. Two hours to bedtime. He shivers again.

At the dinner table, Murray fidgets, pushes his fish sticks around his plate, plays with his grapes, eats some broccoli-cheese rice, sips his juice. He watches the clock. 6:45. Jennifer talks about the Barbie

CD game she wants for her birthday, three weeks away. His father cranes his neck to watch a baseball game on without sound in the next room. His mother listens to Jennifer talk about the Barbie CD and, every few minutes, tells Murray not to play with his food or not to drink so much juice or not to eat only rice.

Murray slowly eats his fish sticks.

After his bath, which he complained about, since he had been in the pool all afternoon, Murray reads a Curious George book with his father. Murray has been brave so far today, but now, as bedtime gets closer, he is beginning to worry. He wants to ask his father, but so often his father says, "Ask your mother," or "I don't know," or "well, sport, that's just the way things are." Murray suspects that his father knows more than he says he does. Maybe he's just too tired to talk about things. They read three books together and it's time for bed.

"Something on your mind, sport?" his father asks as Murray picks up his pillow from the sofa and heads down the hallway toward his room.

Murray stops, thinks about saying something, thinks about sucking his thumb, something he hasn't done in over a year, shakes his head and continues down the hallway.

"I'll send your mother in," his father says.

Murray nods and walks.

His mother is gone, her kiss still cool on his forehead. The evening is a soft glow outside his window. He listens for sounds from Jennifer's room next door, but hears nothing. His mother and father are murmuring at the other end of the house.

Murray doesn't know if his mother would like him sleeping with the Walkman radio. Toys and stuffed animals are okay, but a radio is different. He can use the Walkman in the car on trips and even in the mall after he has run out of quarters for the arcade games, but bed is different, so he doesn't ask, he just waits until he thinks they think he's asleep, then he pulls it from the jumble of things he keeps under the bed, slips the cheap foam earphones over his head and turns the radio on.

Static rustles like a lizard in dry leaves. Something has moved the dial and lost the station. He wheels the tuning dial with his thumb, squinting in the dark at the glowing display, until he hears the crashing organ, the murmur of the crowd in the background, and the familiar voice intone, "Welcome, friends! Hello, friends! Welcome, friends, in the Everlasting and Powerful and Glorious Name of Jesus Christ Crucified and Risen from the Dead! Amen and amen and amen!"

Murray shivers.

Thursday is free time during Arts and Crafts. For the first five minutes, Murray wanders aimlessly among the supplies with most of the other children, eyeing the slowly shrinking heap of crispy clay, the rows of white glue bottles, the yarn, the popsicle sticks, the Styrofoam shapes. By the time he decides, he is left facing a cardboard box of assorted crayons, construction paper, some tempera paint and three different colors of fuzzy pipe cleaners.

Sitting down at the very end of one of the long art tables, Murray shuffles the construction paper until he comes to yellow, then experiments with his half dozen crayons, doodling in the corner, until he decides that forest green shows up best. He starts at the bottom and draws a big rectangle, its solid borders accented with smudges and chunks of crayon, then he attaches a spidery column to one corner of the rectangle. He stops and squints, then widens the column.

"That's better," he says softly.

Ricky Spinoli, who is making an airplane out of popsicle sticks, glue and cotton balls, leans over to look at this rectangle and column, but doesn't say anything. Murray scratches his face and continues.

Another rectangle and another column. A wide, dark column. Murray squints to try and see the image in his mind better, the dimensions and the colors, the shapes. He has never seen in real life what he is trying to draw, but that shouldn't make a difference.

Mrs. Hubert announces that there are ten minutes left in Arts and Crafts. Ricky starts making airplane sounds, picks up his half-completed model and makes a few swooping dives over the end of the table, machine-gunning Murray's rectangles and columns.

"Vrrrrrooooooooooommmmmmmm!" The half plane pulls up from its dive, swoops left and right, does an impossible barrel roll, then returns to the safety of the table top.

"I just bombed your castle," Ricky says. "I blew up all your people."

"It's not a castle," Murray says.

Ricky silently returns to his project. Murray connects the columns to a third, bigger rectangle. The rectangles would look better if they were filled in, especially this one, so he peels the paper from the green crayon, has second thoughts, uses a light blue crayon instead. Using the length of the crayon, he presses wide blue smears across the page, trying not to, but running over the lines, so that the rectangle looks like it is shooting off blue electricity. He chooses red for the smaller rectangles.

When Mrs. Hubert calls time and tells the children to start putting their supplies away, Murray has attached another set of columns to the top of the big rectangle, ovals to the ends of the columns, multi-colored spikes in half circles radiating from the ovals. He wants to color in the ovals, but there is no time. Mrs. Hubert asks the children to put their names on their projects, if they can, and to title them, then she walks around the room behind them, calling out to the rest of the class what each child's creation looks like, if there is no title, or reading the title out loud.

"A motorcycle. Very good, Kenny. Kittens and puppies. Nice job, Ellen. Ooh, a purple dragon race car. That's very colorful,

Bobby. Ricky has made an airplane." Mrs. Hubert looks at Murray's unfinished drawing, then to the title Murray has scrawled along the right side of the construction paper. It looks like Murray has written bily gots, so Mrs. Hubert thinks "Billy Goats Gruff," but the drawing doesn't look like a goat at all, more like the troll in the story, so Mrs. Hubert says, "Very good, Murray, a big green troll."

Murray blinks and looks at this drawing. Mrs. Hubert moves on to the next child.

Troll. Another piece to the puzzle.

Saturday afternoon. Lazy sunshine filters through the trees in the backyard. The lawn, freshly mown, is a festival of mulched grass, of shredded paper and torn plastic wrappers and chopped up grasshoppers, of spiders scurrying with sacks of eggs on their backs. Murray's father swings in a hammock between the maple trees, a can of beer in his hand, a tiny television perched on his stomach. Murray pushes a toy bulldozer up and over the roots of the maple at the foot of the hammock while the faraway insect voice of the baseball announcer drones.

"Come on," Murray's father growls at the tv, then, a few seconds later, says, "Shit!"

Murray's bulldozer pushes a pile of dead leaves against the largest maple root.

"What's the Holy Ghost like?" he says, just as his father jerks in the hammock and says, "Yes!"

Murray waits while his father chortles and takes a long sip of beer. "Ha ha!" his father says to the TV. "Take *that*, Yankees!"

Murray's father acts and sounds different when he's watching baseball games. When a game comes on TV, Murray's mother usually finds something else to do, like shopping or having her hair done.

"What's the Holy Ghost like?" Murray asks again when his father has stopped making sounds from the hammock.

"What?"

"The Holy Ghost," Murray says again.

"What about it?"

"What's the Holy Ghost like?"

"Oh. Well, we don't say 'Holy Ghost,' see? We say 'Holy Spirit.' Big difference." Murray's father winks at him and takes another sip of beer.

Murray stares at him. "What's it like?"

There is silence for a few seconds while Murray's father thinks, then a few more seconds as he finishes the can of beer. Something happens on the TV that makes him jerk again and then let out a long whistle. When he looks down, Murray is still looking back up at him. "Oh. Well, the Holy Spirit is kind of like, well, well, kind of like your grandma."

Murray bulldozes some more leaves.

"Which one? The dead one or the live one?"

His father shrugs. "Either one, I guess."

"Oh."

"Don't worry about that stuff, sport. None of that is really important right now. You're just a kid. You should be worried about baseball. Let the Holy Spirit worry about you, not the other way around. Got it?"

"Okay."

The next day at church, Murray is surprised to hear Pastor Jim mention the Holy Spirit repeatedly during the sermon. He tries to pay attention, but most of the words to him are like wrapped presents under the Christmas tree that are meant for others. He can see them, he can shake them, but until someone else opens them, he won't know what they are. Words words words float over him, like Christmas in a spaceship without gravity. The Holy Spirit will protect you, he hears Pastor Jim say. Have no fear, for the Holy Spirit is with you. Murray floats away, riding on the warm swells of Pastor Jim's honeyed tones, and in his daydream a giant of rectangles and columns and fiery eyes does battle with Grandma Jenkins and Mamo Dupree, who hit him with purses and poke him with knitting needles and throw him to the ground and stomp up and down on him until he gets really angry and jumps up and grabs them by their fat ankles and swings them around until their heads turn blue and pop off.

Murray's mother looks down at him as a sudden shiver catches him.

"Time to stand for the hymn, honey."

Murray does as he's told, terrible images fading behind his eyes.

Murray slips out of bed and finds the Walkman radio in the box at the foot of his bed. He plugs the headphones in and climbs back under the covers. In the dark, he gently thumbs the tuning knob, his ear filling with harsh static and guitars and the lazy voices of baseball game announcers. He slides the knob until he hears the jaunty organ music and familiar laughter, though he doesn't know what there is to laugh about. He shudders as the voice of Reverend Bob starts talking right to him, his voice shrill and jumpy. It sounds sometimes like the man is on fire and trying to finish what he has to say before he gets burned up. Murray shudders and listens to the words coming out in a rush.

"Amen, tell you what there is nothing in the world can stop the power of Him, yes, the Holy Ghost, yes, yes, the Holy Ghost, yes, He's gonna get you, gonna get you, gonna get you and burn you with the fire of conviction and strike you hard, yes, Jesus! Like lightning, like a Holy Sword, yes, like a flaming sword, yes! The Holy Ghost, you can't hide from Him, you can't run from Him, so wide, you can't get around Him, so deep, you can't get under Him, so high, you can't get over Him, if you make your bed in Heaven, He's there, if you make your bed in Hell, He's there, He's everywhere!! He's like a giant walking on the earth, like a, like a, like an Iron Giant of holiness, like a robot of Love and conviction, like a, like a towering Giant of rebuke to the evil and punishment to the wicked. He's a huge flaming spear of justice!!"

Flaming spear, Iron Giant, Robot of Love, Bolt of Lightning. Murray opens his eyes to see the faint glow of the newly risen moon outside his window, then shuts them tight, painfully tight, afraid he'll see the Holy Ghost come flaming through the woods, burning eyes looking for him, a big meaty Holy Hand waiting to pound him into his mattress because he has done something wrong. The closet is closed, so He can't be in there, and Murray checked under the bed, so He can't be there, either, but He's out there somewhere, like Reverend Bob says, and He's coming to get him and no one can save him, not Jennifer, not Daddy, not Mommy, not Pastor Jim.

"He's coming, He's coming, He's coming!" Revered Bob says from out there somewhere in the ambiguous place Murray knows as America. Murray imagines Reverend Bob like a giant himself, Reverend Bob with multiple arms and three mouths, his eyes glowing, his head revolving, atop a mountain, like a radio tower. Below him people are jumping and shouting "Amen!" and "Yes, Jesus!" and shaking their arms over their heads and pointing the way for Reverend Bob so he can send the Holy Ghost, send Him crashing through forests and climbing over mountains, send Him wading through rivers and trampling cities, all the way across the fruity plains and amber graves to Murray, in his bed, in the dark, alone.

The Brick Murder: A Tragedy

Dear Reader, in approximately 7000 words a murder will commence. Murder by brick, to be exact, a messy affair indeed. The terrible event will be the logical conclusion of a series of tragic preconditions, the details of which you shall soon learn. Foreknowledge of the outcome is a standard of classical tragedy, so these facts shouldn't diminish the effect of the following pages. You should still be moved to pity and fear. You might very well experience a catharsis.

Tragedies are special, so special that the Greeks became obsessed about them, building their dramatic literature around those spectacularly anguished and anguishing tales of horror anticipated but not avoidable. They crowded their amphitheaters to squirm in silent delighted dismay as kings and queens drove their proverbial chariots into the ditch. Our saturation media want us to believe that the world around us is full of tragedies, that we live in a tragic place at a tragic time. A blind man walks through an opened elevator door and tumbles 45 stories to his untimely end: *Blind Man Falls to Tragic Death*. A toddler gets mangled by a riding mower: *Toddler*

Dies in Tragic Accident. An engine falls off a plane and two hundred people are transformed into elaborate pieces of barbeque: *Tragedy Strikes Los Angeles-Bound Flight.* Little Leonard crawls into the deep end of a swimming pool while Mommy stares glassy-eyed at *General Hospital,* the day's third vodka and tonic in hand: *Mom Drunk While Infant Tragically Drowns.* Tragic mishaps all, the TV newsreaders would have us believe. But our dictionaries tell us that these things are not tragedies. Most bad things are just that—bad things.

But not *The Brick Murder.* I am pleased, therefore, to present the following classically tragic tale in the hopes of being both instructive and admonitory, to teach and to warn.

According to conventions dating back to Aristotle, tragedies must satisfy several criteria, most of which are sadly lacking when, for instance, the late night maintenance man at McDonald's falls head first into the deep fat fryer reclaim vat and drowns in 10 gallons of rancid rendered animal fat. This is a bad thing, a very bad thing (not least for McDonald's, which must suffer 17 days of suppressed earnings and bad publicity[4]), but it is not tragic because:

The person involved was not "of high estate" (usually a king in the old days, but we can replace "high estate" with "of some importance," say, a CEO, a doctor, even a college professor; but face it, a McDonald's maintenance man, unless he happens to be the recently deposed monarch of some Eastern European duchy named Urbithia or Strovsloslovia, is not even remotely a person of high estate).

The resulting mishap was not inevitable, but could have been avoided.

The mishap did not have consequences for others beyond the mere scope of the person's family, such as was the case with

---

[4] The median duration of "customer avoidance due to negative media issues regarding illness, dismemberment or death at a fast food chain" according to Robicheaux, Lazlo and Rensellaer, Inc., Meme is the Message Media Consultants.

the McDonald's maintenance man, unless, say, his untimely death triggered a constitutional or succession crisis in Urbithia or Strovsloslovia, or discord among competing Urbithian or Strovsloslovian exiles living in adjacent neighborhoods in Milwaukee; and

The resulting mishap was not the consequence of this person's great flaw, which also, ironically, is most often this person's greatest personal attribute (craftiness, ambition, pride, greed, honor) but merely poor timing, alcohol, drugs, or our old friend, just plain bad luck.

The Brick Murder, as it was eventually, and not incidentally, in a perverse way, quite affectionately called, satisfied the classical criteria robustly; it was, in fact, the real deal.

To wit:

The Players of High Estate:

Brigadier General Darius Cromwell Butterbean, USA (retired). ROTC Eastern Texas College of Christ. Veteran of Vietnam, Panama and the Gulf War I, winner of three Purple Hearts, two Bronze Stars and a Silver Star; President of the Southern Christian Military College of the South; Dean of the Faculty, Old Dominion Military Academy, and adjunct member of the English Department, ODMA, speciality: the Literature of War, alternately referred to by his less-than-impressed colleagues as "Bombs and Books."

Harwell Larouche, Ph.D., University of Wisconsin, Early 20th Century American Literature specialist, with sub-specialty in African-American Literature, author of the seminal study on Sherwood Anderson, *A Fevered Mind*, Associate Professor, Department of English, ODMA. Military service, none. A semi-secret fractional Negro.

The sense of inevitability:

All witnesses to *The Brick Murder* (there were no eyewitnesses to the murder, but plenty of folks heard it, folks who could have, in the words of Mrs. Gladiola Butterbean and the State Police investigating officer, "done *something* about it," but, for reasons not quite clear, chose *not* to) and victims of its regrettably untidy aftermath—all the members of the English Department, most members of the general faculty and the administration, scores of students, the janitorial staff—when asked their thoughts afterward, remarked, in language remarkably similar, something to the effect of, "We should have seen it coming." In truth, many of them did see it coming (the signs were all there) but phrasing it that way—"We should have seen it coming"—let them off the hook, they seemed to feel. Many people saw it coming, but felt, paradoxically, that there really wasn't anything they could have done, short of committing the murder him or herself, to prevent that very particular murder from happening. What fate wants, fate gets.

Consequences Whose Scope Extends Beyond the Affected Individuals and Their Immediate Families:

This, perhaps, is the most profound manner in which *The Brick Murder* satisfies the classical requirements of the tragic event, for the consequences were legion.

First, the Academy had to search for a new dean, no small undertaking, given that the former dean, in the third year of his five-year contract, had embarked upon an extremely ambitious program of "academic renewal" that involved a painful, protracted and confusing reorganization of administrative and support staff, the hiring and firing of faculty, the inauguration of several new academic programs and the planned construction of three new buildings. Two associate and one assistant dean had been newly hired, having been sold on the "academic renewal" of ODMA and now, in late August, the week of The Brick Murder, these people were on their way from recently sold homes in Idaho, Texas and Florida, heading straight into an administrative and academic vortex of uncertainty, recrimination and "payback time," as all demises of deans, real or institutional, inevitably entail. And 43 students pre-registered for "Bombs and Books" had to look for another course to fulfill enrollment requirements. Many more students, enrolled in the courses of Professor Larouche, were similarly inconvenienced. Many matters were in a state of flux, and the acting dean would have to be adept at keeping many balls in the air simultaneously.

Second, the Academy had to search for a new Early 20th Century American Literature specialist, preferably an African-American one, otherwise, "the numbers wouldn't be right."[5]

Third, the local NAACP chapter lost its most prominent member in higher education.

Fourth, the local PBS affiliate, which was set to feature Professor Larouche's new book on Willa Cather and Nella Larsen in its Regional Authors Program, now had a gaping hole to fill in the 5th installment of the weekly, hour-long series.

Fifth, other members of the English Department would have to look elsewhere to enhance their personal databases on "Things Educated and Negro."

The Tragic Flaws:
1) The inability to keep one's fucking mouth shut.
2) Anger, insecurity, and pride commingling to create an intense propensity to overcompensate ad seething resentment.

The Inability to "Keep One's Fucking Mouth Shut":
General Butterbean had made a career for himself in the Army of speaking out when others were silent. Sometimes this meant challenging conventional thinking on tactics and strategy, which turned out to be successful in averting disaster on the battlefield and

---

[5] Colonel Rayborn Rimley, Virginia Militia Unorganized, Dept. Head, English and Fine Arts, in memo to Acting Dean Colonel Frank Furber, September 30, 2005.

saving lives. Other times this meant taking a little too long to suck up, kiss ass or brown nose superior officers, and would lead fellow grade officers to lean over during protracted meetings and say to him, "why can't you just keep your fucking mouth shut so we can get the hell out of here?" And, as a young officer in Vietnam, he ignored the advice/directive to "keep your fucking mouth shut" and reported some "irregular and inappropriate treatment of civilian non-combatants" in a small village in Yuan Then hamlet. The resultant publicity advanced his name in the public eye. Not a few of his colleagues hated him for helping to bring disgrace upon the Army, as they saw it (massacres happened all the time in war; they were only 'notable' when the press found out about them) but he attracted enough attention in Washington that his career was assured.

Anger, Insecurity, and Pride Commingling To Create an Intense Propensity To Overcompensate:

Being a self-styled quasi-African-American[6], Professor Larouch lived a life of anxiety, compensation, paranoia, anger and overachievement. He had passed most of his life first not knowing he was doing so, then semi-consciously, and, finally, fully cognizant, and then, when necessity demanded, coming out of the racial closet in order to get a job. During this latter stage of passing, he felt two kinds of guilt: the first consisting in shame that he was

---

[6] Professor Larouche made a quixotic career out of challenging the conventional wisdom of the designation "African-American." In "How Many Colors in the Rainbow?" an op-ed piece for the Baltimore Sun, he mused, "At what point does one become African-American, and not something else? $1/64^{th}$? $1/128^{th}$? $1/256^{th}$? And when one becomes African-American, does one un-become Hungarian-, Polish-, or Ukrainian-American? This is not purely an academic question. I have seen the oh-so-subtle realignment of the racial calculus behind the eyes of colleagues, acquaintances, "friends," when they learn of a heretofore unsuspected African-American's African-Americanness. 'Oh. I thought you were Greek!'" [Professor Larouche himself was, by his own reckoning, $1/16^{th}$ African-American

denying a part of his family, his heritage, his history,[7] cutting ties, however tenuous, to a past rich in suffering and significance; the other consisting in fear the he would be found out, revealed for what he was, racially outed, and that this would cause the very fabric of the universe, vis-à-vis himself, to change in ways both measurable and inscrutable. His sense of self, dependent in no small part upon what sense of him others held, would be changed, would now constantly be in turmoil, in fact, because every person who would now have to re-know him, would have a slightly different opinion of him, or so he imagined, and so every new encounter would be fraught with uncertainty, second-guessing, suspicion, fear, interpretation, paranoia. ("Larouche? Very well spoken, don't you think? [For a Negro!]" "I always thought he had a slight accent, kind of a southern thing he was trying to hide." "Nigger." "You been down in the locker room with him after squash. Does he have a big dick?" "Why did he try to hide it for so long?" He particularly loathed it when people started calling him "brother." And so on.) And then, of course, he could no longer be a spy in the house of race (one of his, and perhaps his very best, justification for keeping his secret; or at least, this is what he told himself). Being such a spy, or a double agent, a faux white guy, or faux whitish guy, a quasi-Caucasian, he was privy to what he termed to himself in mental italics The Unguarded Moments of White People—friends, acquaintances, lovers—regarding matters of race. Why, he was one of them, so they could casually, occasionally (and to their credit, some, never) say things to him that they would never, ever say to a true black person.[8] This, naturally, presented problems. For one

---

[7] Even though, to be honest, he knew as much about his biological father's family as his mother did, which was next to nothing. It was the intellectual *concept* of loss that affected him.

[8] This was a complicated matter, naturally. Some comments were outright racist, while others were more subtle, consisting of code words, inflections, body language, significant looks. It was, at times, quite mentally demanding.

thing, as one woman he was dating pointed out to him, what was he a spy *for*? What would he ever *do* with the information? Many of the people he knew were so deeply ensconced in the bosom of institutional racism that they were unaware of their prejudices, he answered. *Okay. So what? What are you going to do?* He didn't know, and being put on the spot in such a fashion, being made to think of what he might actually do, irked him. As an academic, he was trained more to think than to do. He could never give her a sufficient answer, one of the reasons why, he suspected, she later left him. But it was valuable information he was compiling. For example: the head of the Anthropology Department at Kansas State would do Al Jolson impressions, or, at cocktail parties, would make snide sotto voce remarks to Larouche about Southern Blacks whom he felt to be intellectually *wanting*; the adjunct technical writing specialist at Pittsburgh Polytechnic, who, when speaking about Black people, would lower her voice, as though one of them might be *justaroundthecorner* listening, getting mad, preparing to (in a predatory sexual way) *POUNCE*; or how, if a class happened to be all-white, and issues of race would come up, the class would feel free to use the worst stereotypes about African-Americans. *And?*

"I will write a book someday," he had said to this woman as they ate raspberry sorbet one night. "It will be an angry indictment of the race hypocrites."

"Better do it soon," the former lover had said. "Only young men can write angry novels and get away with it."

"Okay," he had said. And he had started the novel, gotten fifteen pages into it, set it aside for a year, turned it into a play, then a script (that's where the real money was anyway; and face it, in writing this exposé he would be burning plenty of bridges and there was nothing better to cross a river whose bridge had been burnt than a raft made out of money), then back into a novel again. But he stayed angry, the writing was not therapeutic, and he continued to overachieve, as he had done all his life, in part because he knew that once his secret got out, and it always, inevitably did (at Kansas, at Pittsburgh, at SUNY Binghamton), people would look for excuses to justify their racist reactions to him.

The novel was still "in-progress." "I am writing a novel," he would tell people when they asked him what he was up to. "Oh, what's it about?" people would ask. "It's speculative fiction about race and identity," he would say, and, "it's hard to put into a nutshell." The term "speculative fiction" would stop conversation as though he had announced he was writing it with ink fashioned from fermenting turds. "Oh," people would say. "Well, I look forward to reading it." Right, he would think, and, eventually add, almost in spite of himself, *whitey.*

He didn't use or think the term "whitey" very often. After all, he was mostly white himself, had grown up in a white neighborhood with white parents and white friends and white girlfriends. He was only slightly olive-complected. But he had learned over time that to Super White People, as he called them, those WASPS and other white people who looked for all the world unblemished with unwhite blood, who could provide you a genealogical tree that began with two Cro Magnons in Germany, everybody else—Irish, Italian, French, Belgian, you name it—weren't really the right kind of white. These were the ultimate whiteys.

Sometimes he would look at himself in the mirror, try to see himself as, he believed, others sometimes saw him, would get agitated, confused, resentful. His brow would tighten, his mouth crimp, and he would say things like, "I am a cauldron of seething anxiety and resentment." Then he would not smile.

He had finally, purposefully, come out of the racial closet for the ODMA job. Tenure had eluded him in Pittsburgh and he wasn't getting any younger, so he was grasping for anything remotely resembling a brass ring. The ODMA job description had been written in academic code for Negroes or other qualifying racial or ethnic minorities.[9] He had, with difficulty, written African-American under *race* on the application, a first for him. The end result of this: one angry motherfucker.

The Brick:

General Darius Cromwell Butterbean had spent most of his career as an artillery officer. Artillery, according to the Army, is the "King of Battle," its job "to kill people and break things." Butterbean could never really know how many people he had actually killed, wounded, maimed or psychologically scarred for life, since most of his killings had been done over long, sometimes ridiculously long, distances, but whenever he had a chance, and could be reasonably certain of his responsibility, he would collect pieces of things his artillery had broken. Most of these things had been buildings made from some kind of brick. So his particular military fetish collection was a series of Third World bricks (just for the hell of it he had a friend bring him some Kosovo brick, even though by then he was out of the Army and into academia and despite the fact that the Army had not fired a single artillery shell during that "conflict" [all concrete, cement, brick, steel, iron, stone, wood and otherwise constructed buildings had been destroyed by Air Force bombs and missiles and Navy ship-launched cruise missiles]) that varied in color, texture, weight and density. These chunks of brick sat on the credenza in his office, each with a small engraved bronze label and mounted on a piece of varnished wood. Bricks. Just bricks. This made people ask him about them, of course, and he could and would launch into a disquisition about the Army, the Artillery, history of, tactics of, special kinds of, breaking things "with extreme prejudice,

---

[9] ODMA was a school with a long, distinguished history of military accomplishments and an equally long, dubious history of racial accommodation. In 173 years of higher education, a total of 430 man-hours of non-white instruction had been logged. It was, as Board of Visitors Chairman, Chandler "Newt" Newton VI said, in an April 12, 2001, meeting, "high time for the situation to be studied by an executive committee."

har har!!," the process of brick-making in Vietnam, Laos, Cambodia, Panama, Kuwait, Iraq and other countries. He would fail to explain the conspicuous stains on some of the bricks.

General Butterbean had majored in English at Eastern Texas College of Christ while an ROTC cadet, and during one of his stateside postings had earned a Master's degree from the University of Southwestern Texas—El Paso. His Ph.D. in English Education Administration had been conferred by Eastern Delaware State, which had a program particularly suited to armed services veterans in academe who needed that last degree to get them "over the top." Most of his career outside the military had been in administration, although he had taught a freshman comp class here and there, and an occasional American literature survey. He had been hired at ODMA to be Dean of the Faculty with no consideration for his teaching abilities, but then had wrangled a position for himself in the English Department teaching The Literature of War, or what his "colleagues" called, behind his back, Bombs and Books. It was not a serious literature course, the inclusion of *The Red Badge of Courage* and *All Quiet on the Western Front* notwithstanding. Most of the novels and short stories that appeared on the syllabus were of the techno-thriller variety about stolen nuclear warheads or biotoxins on the market to the highest beady-eyed Muslim bidder, or tales of special operations warfare written by former Navy SEALS. Through his discretionary fund as Dean, he was often able to bring the authors of these books to campus, sometimes in bunches of two or three, and class would consist of three retired military men telling war stories to enraptured students. The cadets ate it up. They got to read books about things getting blown up on a regular basis. General Butterbean's student evaluations, for the two semesters he taught the course, were "off the charts." "The books are so reel [sic] you can almost smel [sic] the napom [sic]" and "I liked how the books made you feel you are really in combat the smells and stuff," were representative of the comments cadets wrote on the evaluations that the Dean, as Dean, would read about himself as professor.

Timeline:

Professor Larouche had been teaching at ODMA for eleven long, generally unhappy years. It was hard for him to be happy in a place that, he felt, required him to compromise an essential part of himself each day, namely, his integrity. He was required to wear a uniform, something he had at first considered an amusing eccentricity (and a compromise he was willing to make in order to get a job in a very tight market) but which he now considered as an act of complicity with the global imperialistic war machine that the United States had finally, unequivocally, inevitably, revealed itself to be. The uniform he was compelled to wear was a standard United States Army officer's uniform. He put it on in the morning at home, wore it to school, then wore it home in the afternoon. Often, at the various convenience stores where he stopped for gasoline or coffee, the uniform would elicit comments. Mostly, people would treat him deferentially, holding doors, imploring him to cut in line. Once, a well-groomed man about his age (45) shook his hand and thanked him for all he "was doing for our country." "I'm teaching English," Larouche had replied, and the man had looked confused, then smiled sheepishly and gone away. What Larouche feared was that someone with a bone to pick with the Army, or the United States in general, would see him as a "soft" target. Someday someone would take out all their anger at the Army or the government on *him*.

But the uniform was not the key source of the unhappiness. There were other, more immediate and pressing sources. His students were, largely, uninterested in learning, looking merely to "get their tickets punched," as one of his senior colleagues had expressed it. The department, once poor, was now merely mediocre, filled with half-hearted scholars who realized with a 4/4 teaching load they could never get any serious scholarship done, and so had ceased doing it; and knew that since the school was not a particularly good academic institution, that others would not be beating down the doors to get in; and, further, since they had no real records of achievement, they were essentially unemployable at the same pay anywhere else. In short, their jobs were safe if they wanted them, and all they had to do was wear the uniform, not question authority, teach uninterested students and, every once in a while, publish a book review; and if they wanted to go elsewhere, their choices were junior colleges or high schools. This was the status quo until, Larouche maintained, he applied for promotion to full professor ten years after his arrival. Then, suddenly, standards got tougher, the bar was lifted, and he found himself having to do more and be more than the people whose offices he had to pass to and from class every day. In the course of the Dean's "academic renewal," occasioned in no small part by the micro-managing of the state's Council on Higher Education, which had been created by an activist Republican governor at the behest of state representatives in the thrall, and pay, of powerful business interests who wished for "business models" to be more closely adhered to in academe, a complex welter of assessments, evaluations and benchmarks had been instituted, and in order for these various "tools" to be implemented, calibrated, correlated and adjudicated, a highly refined, multi-tiered system of faculty performance analysis had to be developed. In his blacker moods, Larouche would be inclined to agree that his ass was getting micro-managed, assessed, implemented, calibrated, correlated, adjudicated and analyzed like there was no tomorrow. He was being lynched by analysis. And he imagined his elder peers, all white, all inferior scholars, but all full professors and all making many thousands a year more than he, were laughing at him.

General Butterbean, as the Chief Academic Officer of Old Dominion Military Academy, was beyond the grip of the Evaluation Machine, and so, though his classes were, from all reports, gab sessions with veterans and breathless reviews of shoot-'em-up war glorification potboilers, he commanded an inviolable slot on the academic schedule each semester for his popular course. Though he had no seniority in the department other than his general's star, he wielded the kind of death grip on schedule slots that 30-year tenured full professors did at Yale or Princeton. So "Bombs and Books" was taught each semester, Tuesday/Thursday, 0930 in Liberal Arts 201, the department library, a conference room with the requisite twenty-foot-long table. This was not a problem until the Fall of 2005, when, due to an enrollment oversight by the new registrar using the new automated registration system, twice as many students were registered for "Bombs and Books" as the class could hold. Butterbean was flattered by the enrollment numbers and, due to some "academic renewal" downtown in his schedule thanks to "cyclical reorientation," as he explained in a memo to the department chair, he could actually afford the time to teach two classes. The problem was that adding another B&B meant removing someone else's course.

Larouche had taught twelve different courses in his eleven years at ODMA. For three years he had been planning on teaching a course on Contemporary African-American Literature, naturally with some trepidation. One of the more prevalent memes in academe was that those best suited to teaching African-American literature were African-Americans themselves, an essentialist notion that, of course, was both insightful and irrational, so such a course had never been proposed, let alone taught, at ODMA. But with the arrival of Larouche, that all changed. He had proposed in early Spring to teach the class, the proposal had been accepted by the curriculum committee, and the assistant professor in charge of scheduling had put it on the master schedule for Fall 2005. But even though he had applied for the job as an African-American, he had managed to remain a stealth Negro by dint of his 15/16 Caucasian qualifications, lack of "Black accent," "Good hair," and whatnot. Certainly, each succeeding year of new students didn't know he was a "One drop Nigger," and only became aware of this when he told them so, not necessarily in those words.

The week before classes began for the Fall Semester, Larouche was called into the office of Colonel Stilton Rimley, Victorian lit specialist and chairman of the department. Pleasantries were exchanged for 45 seconds. Colonel Rimley, a native of Savannah, Georgia, had inherited from his mother that unique and disarming way cultured Savannah women had of conducting unpleasant business with the minimum of fuss and stress. After the pleasantries were completed, he lowered his voice 10 decibels and asked Larouche to close his office door.

Larouche knew this meant that he was, in some way, fucked. In less time than it would take to read "The Windhover." Colonel Rimley explained, in a sing-song voice barely above a whisper, that General Butterbean would be teaching an additional section of "Bombs and Books" and that Larouche would not be teaching Contemporary African-American Literature after all, but would instead be teaching a second composition course, replacing one of the adjuncts, who would teach only three comp sections instead of four.

Larouche was not stunned, exactly, but he was surprised. His almost-immediate, irrational, thought was to leap across the corner of desk that separated him from his department chair and throttle the man, and in shamefully imagining himself doing it—the thwack of the corner of the desk against his thigh as he lunged toward Rimley, the inarticulate gasp dying in the other man's throat, papers flying into the air and settling haphazardly onto the floor, the phone being knocked from the hook, Rimley's ineffectual, too-late attempt to shield himself from harm with his fleshy forearms, the look of shock on his face, the bulging eyes, the softness of muscle and brittle cartilage under Larouche's thumbs as he crushed the man's throat, the unbelievable surge of adrenaline—he realized that this certainly would fuck up his hoped-for promotion. He shook his head.

"I've—I've been planning that course for years," he said. "I have arranged for August Wilson and Yusef Komunyakaa to visit class. I've even got—I've got a verbal commitment from Percival Everett."

Colonel Rimley blinked. Larouche doubted that the man had ever heard of these writers before, though Wilson and Komunyakaa had commanded three Pulitzers and a National Book Award. When Rimley was uncertain or in the dark about a matter or caught in a lie, he would maintain a pleasant silence for several long seconds, then follow with a non sequitur.

"Sounds like a medieval name," he said, smiling. "Well, I guess we'll have to make arrangements about that." His eyes were convincingly sympathetic.

Arrangements. Larouche snorted, though not too loudly. How many times through the years had white folks let themselves off the hook after creating chaos in the lives of black folks with words like "arrangements"? Accidentally kill someone with an errant shotgun blast while they were washing dishes? Make an arrangement. Run over a child chasing a ball into the street? Arrange something. Sell a family downriver? That could be arranged. The brief history flashback resurrected the anger he had felt initially, magnified it, and he once again imagined himself "Going Ghetto Ass" on the little man. He had experienced unreasoning anger before, times at which he had felt restraint being peeled away from him like sloughed-off skin, but "Going Ghetto Ass" was a variety of anger particular to black people, or so the comedian on Comedy Central who had first acquainted him with the phrase had stated. To truly go "Ghetto Ass" on someone, a person had to actually be from the ghetto, or if not from a city large enough to house a ghetto, at least from "the wrong side of the tracks." Larouche didn't qualify on either of these grounds, but, given his fractional pedigree, he felt it was still within him to get in touch with his inner Negro and go "Ghetto Ass." This didn't necessarily mean throttling, but did imply cursing abundantly and creatively, accusing people of racism and, in the words of the Comedy Central comedian, "throwing other people's shit around and fucking up they crib." Rimley had plenty of memorabilia, most of it small original printings of Tennyson's and Swinbourne's poetry, some old original photographs of Browning that could be knocked from his desk in spectacular "Ghetto Ass" fashion. And Larouche wouldn't just knock these things down, either. He would obliterate them.

Larouche thought again of his promotion, which had been denied the previous year because, in the words of Colonel Rimley, he hadn't served on a sufficient number of Academy-wide committees, and, therefore, wasn't widely enough known on Post, particularly, it was felt, among the senior faculty on the tenure and promotions committee. Choking your department head would certainly take care of the latter, but it would also permanently ruin his chances for promotion and a $10,000 a year raise.

"Well . . . darn," he said. He tried to formulate several arguments against this most egregious fucking he was receiving, but his mind just hummed like, he later explained to his lawyer, the buzzing of a dying fly trapped between the panes of a storm window on a summer's day. Profanity in academia, unless used ironically in a monograph full of footnotes, was verboten. But profanity was all that would come to mind. He wanted to blister the wall paint with a masterful barrage of the most obscene words he could string together. Instead he just said, "This is just . . . okay. Well."

And he left, seething. Larouche had only slightly more contact with General Butterbean than had other members of the faculty, but those who knew both of them agreed they were a definite oil and water pair. Since Butterbean was a nominal member of the department he did have an office (larger than Larouche's) on the same floor. Occasionally Butterbean would appear in the hallways, greeting people in his ridiculously loud voice, asking them how they were and guffawing out of all proportion to simple replies like, "Just fine, General." Most of Larouche's contacts with the man were in the subservient position of faculty member vis a vis a dean. There were numerous e-mail memos, military fashion, detailing advances in the Academic Renewal Campaign as though they were the skirmishes and battles of an actual war. Then there were the episodes of what Major Thurman Yancey, a nominal friend of Larouche's in History, would call "Psycho Shouting." Several times over his three-year tenure at the Academy, Butterbean had "gone ballistic" in meetings with faculty, and the results had not been pretty. Spittle flew, scarred fists pounded conference tables, decibels rose. Larouche had been to two such meetings and had had the courage (some said the temerity) to challenge the General's verbal onslaughts with reasoned questions, although, admittedly, from a row far enough back in the general meeting that the General couldn't positively identify him. Butterbean's saving grace was that he never shouted directly at women and never used profanity. Had he done either of these, Yancey and others felt, he would have been long gone, disposed of by a Board of Visitors which was loathe to countenance "unseemly or ungentlemanly behavior." As it was, Butterbean stayed within the boundaries of acceptable behavior and persisted in brow-beating and terrifying his faculty with closed-door beratings, acidic e-mails and ferocious, silent scowls, but not a few people felt that he might actually do physical harm to someone if pushed to the edge. After all, the man had been a highly trained killer for most of his professional life.

Leaving his "meeting" with Rimley that day, Larouche passed Butterbean's office. The door was closed, so Larouche stood and looked at it, noticing the class schedule/office hour card for the upcoming semester, and saw that Butterbean had already written in two sessions of Bombs and Books and one hour per week of office time for student consultations. Larouche thought of his own schedule card, which still lay on his desk. He hadn't written anything on it yet, but he had imagined many times how that schedule card would look, with Contemporary American Literature reduced to Cont. AfroAm Lit to make it fit the narrow space allotted for it. TR 1300-1415. He thought of the syllabus on his C: drive, the hundreds of hours of reading and research that had gone into pruning his required readings to a manageable list, the hours he had spent just on tweaking the syllabus on the computer, moving writers around to make sure that they fit in well with each other and accommodated the vagaries of the ODMA schedule, with its forced marches, military field training exercises, required-attendance athletic events, and so on. He thought of the film crew from the local PBS affiliate that was scheduled to come to his class in three weeks to shoot footage of him teaching for the segment of their documentary about him. He thought of the faithful students of his who had asked for the class over several semesters. He thought of all the ass-kissing he had had to do to get August Wilson to agree to come to a traditionally racist southern military college.

"Yaaar!" someone shouted from behind the door. It sounded like someone belching and doing deep knee bends at the same time.

Larouche leaned closer, his head touching the door, and it swung open.

"Who's there?" the voice came again, louder.

Larouche thought of turning and quickly walking away, but something (fate?) compelled him to push the door open farther and enter.

General Butterbean was on the phone, guffawing. He saw Larouche and waved him in. Larouche took several steps into the office. It was jammed with military memorabilia, as was the General's office in Leavitt Hall, the Administration Building. When you're a general that long, you collect a lot of shit, Larouche guessed. There was one bookshelf along the nearest wall. It was half full. Larouche casually glanced at the books. Rudyard Kipling. Tennyson. Hemingway, and a bunch of Bombs and Books crap. He gritted his teeth.

Butterbean growled something into the phone that sounded like "Arrrseelay!" and hung up. He guffawed at Larouche and asked, "You still around here?"

"Pardon me?"

If Larouche had spent more time around General Butterbean in the Administrative Offices he would have known that this was the General's familiar greeting, a holdover from his active duty Army days, when it was something of a tradition to use the phrase with junior officers. It was a harmless expression, playful jousting, but Larouche suspected something more sinister. A Freudian slip about knowledge of a future event? Did Butterbean know something about what lay in store for Larouche? Were the wheels of Academic Renewal turning to turn him out?

"Almost time to get started around here!" Butterbean said.

"Yes," Larouche said.

"Let me ask you a question!" the General shouted, and beckoned Larouche closer.

"Yes?"

Larouche didn't realize how angry he was at life in general until he stood three feet away from the massive desk and saw up close the collection of bricks arrayed along its front edge that he had often glimpsed from the hallway. In a kind of mystical moment he connected his own shattered hopes for the semester with the remains of shattered Third World buildings he saw before him. He imagined sitting in a simple straw brick and mud dwelling in Iraq and then, in a puff of dust and a concussive shock, looking around to see his family turned into shredded meat and pulverized bone and his home gone. Buh-LAM, as the comic books would render it. He imagined the artillerymen who had wreaked such faraway devastation high-fiving each other from the safety of their position several miles away and saying, "Yar!!" and "Booyah!" to each other.

"How's morale around this place?" Butterbean said.

"Morale?"

"People happy?"

Larouche fumbled for something to say. How could he speak for the hundred or so faculty?

"Every organization gets into a rut! Things need to be shaken up a bit!!"

"Like 'Academic Renewal'?" Larouche said woodenly.

Butterbean slapped his palm on his desk so forcefully that his brick collection jumped.

"That's right!" he said. "Academic Renewal! Academic Renewal is like, is like making an omelet. You like omelets?"

"What? I—I—"

"I love omelets! I love making omelets. Hell, I love making them more than eating them!" Larouche imagined the General in his Army uniform complete with a poofy chef's hat. He snorted.

Larouche was standing close enough to the desk to touch a piece of shattered brick. The bronze plaque read, "Abu Salaam, Iraq, March 20, 1991."

"Make an omelet, you break some eggs, am I right or am I right?"

Larouche found his mouth as dry as dust. He croaked unintelligibly.

"Yar!" Butterbean said.

Since it was a week before classes began, neither the faculty nor the administration were required to be in uniform, but Butterbean was in his. Heavily starched, creased to near cutting sharpness, it sported a mass of ribbons and medals above the left breast pocket.

"I'm having fun, let me tell you!" he said, swiveling in his chair and looking out his window, which gave a view southeast from the building over a landscaped swath of emerald grass and mimosa trees. Larouche's window looked out over the HVAC equipment in a small cement courtyard at the back of the building. Whenever the air conditioning or the heat went on, the bulldozer-sized piece of equipment out there growled and shuddered and Larouche felt the vibrations in his teeth.

"Beats getting shot at, let me tell you!"

"I'm sure it does," Larouche said.

"Oh, that's right, boy," the General said.

"What?" Larouche said.

But the General did not answer.

"I'm making some enemies around here, I'm sure," Butterbean said, "but if you don't make any enemies, you must not be doing your job, my mother used to say!"

Larouche looked at the bookshelf again because there was nowhere else to look and read titles like: *Duty Before Dawn* and *Strike Force Nine!* and *The Equalizers*.

Butterbean swiveled back in his chair and saw Larouche looking at the bookshelf.

"Those are the books for my class! Yeah, it's real popular, real popular!"

"That's what I hear," Larouche said, and then, to his own surprise, heard himself say, "so is masturbation."

The General gave him a confused look, then turned his eyes back to the bookshelf.

"The men love literature that speaks to their experiences!" he said. "The real deal, the gist of life, the blood and bone!" He was silent for several seconds. "None of this namby pamby feel-good stuff!"

Real deal? Namby pamby?

"Hell, some of the crap I saw on the course offerings—" The General broke off in mid-sentence and dismissively waved.

Larouche saw his course float away on the insubstantial puff of air created by the General's backward-jerking hand. He saw his promotion float away.

The General looked at him, and it became obvious to Larouche that the man had no idea who he was. Without his uniform and his name tag, he was, to the General, an anonymous cog in the academic machinery.

"War is eternal," the General said, somewhat wistfully, Larouche thought. The General's hard eyes stared through him. "Part of the eternal character of man. Ignoble at times, yes, but what isn't?"

Larouche opened his mouth, then closed it.

The General looked at a piece of paper on his desk. He snorted.

"I mean, take this Negro Literature class. Yes, okay, the coloreds have had it hard, but who hasn't? Get over it! Get off the high horse!"

Larouche thought he heard something creaking, like time stopping, like the lens of eternity focused suddenly on this small (but still larger than his) space.

"What—what the hell do you mean?" Larouche laughed nervously.

The General picked up the piece of paper and peered at it, pronouncing carefully, "Contemporary African-American Literature. Literature?"

Larouche laughed again. "Are you—are you fucking serious?" he said.

At Larouche's tone, General Butterbean regarded him with that confused look again, his mouth twitching. Larouche felt his scrotum tighten when he saw the man, fifteen years his senior but still imposing, rise.

Larouche saw his own hand grabbing a piece of Abu Salaam and thought: no/yes/no/yes. No promotion. No life. Shit. Motherrucker. "*Negro*"? "*Coloreds*"? "*High horse*"?

"Hey, who the hell are you, anyway?" the General demanded.

Larouche said—and in speaking had the momentary experience of stepping outside of his body and seeing himself from a few inches above and beside his head—"I am a cauldron of seething anger and resentment."

Then he hit the General in the forehead with the brick.

Dust exploded from the impact. Bits of brick flew. General Butterbean's head recoiled and the rest of his body jerked as though he'd been hit with a jolt of electricity. He stared at Larouche, rocking on his heels.

Fuck, Larouche thought.

"Yar!" the General said, and Larouche reared back and hit him again.

I'm killing a man with a brick, he thought as his arm vibrated from the force of the second and third blows, and then, when something warm and wet splashed against his face, he also thought, Most ghettoes are built of brick.

The General, his eyes bulging, raised his arms, hands curled in what Larouche could only imagine was some kind of Army-certified throat-crushing death grip, and bared his teeth—maybe he was going to yell something—but Larouche hit him in the mouth with the remaining wedge of the brick, obliterating exposed teeth, and rose up over the desk to drive the older man into the carpet. The air rushed out of the General's lungs. Larouche heard someone shouting and realized he was hearing his own voice as he continued to wield the brick.

"How you—how you like—how you like—your—your—omelets—omelets—now? Huh? Huh? Huh? How—you—like—your—your—your—omelets? Whitey? How—you—like—them—now? Like—them—now?"

And it went on like that, Colonel Rimley later told reporters, "For a very long time."[10]

---

[10] To Colonel Rimley it may have seemed like a very long time, since his office adjoined the General's, and since he heard the murder with only six inches of wall between him and the ghastly event, but, in fact, the act took only a minute. But a minute, when someone is killing you with a brick, can be a very long time indeed.

Serving a 25- to 40-year sentence with the possibility of parole in 12,[11] Larouche had plenty of time to write. Converting to Islam (it seemed the prudent thing to do to avoid trouble among the various factions running amok in prison; though he could have passed for white, there seemed no distinct advantage in that direction, seeing as how the Black Muslims were greater in number and fiercer in loyalty) he learned Arabic, read the Koran in the original, and then produced a series of papers on Shakespeare's tragedies from a Muslim perspective. Several Muslim literary scholars began correspondence with him, nearly all agreeing that they thought Larouche's insights, though "inspired," "illuminating" and "profound in their scholarship," were a bit too impassioned sometimes, perhaps, as one of them wrote, "just a little bit too angry."

---

[11]Larouche had escaped a first degree murder charge by virtue of the brick, which he had not brought with him. Using a weapon of opportunity in the heat of the moment, especially a weapon not normally associated with murder, and with which Larouche could not be said to be proficient at using for that purpose, did not constitute premeditation. The fact that school had not started yet and that General Butterbean was not in the habit of occupying his English Department office before the opening of school meant that there was no possible way for Larouche to know that Butterbean would be there that day, further limiting the possibilities of premeditation. The damage he had done to the General's head, though, had almost mitigated against him when the judge handed down the sentence. "You may not have formulated a plan in advance," Judge Thorton Weebler said, "but you sure were enthusiastic about carrying it out once you got down to business."

Kurt Jose Ayau

At a Loss for Words

It was a crisis. We were desperate. What can I tell you? I believe in telling the truth, so I'm not going to kid you and say that we had a choice. We didn't. So we had to go see him.

We knew where he lived. Everyone did. Long after he had dropped out of action, no longer in the streets, absent from the barricades, he had still held sway over every counter-culture movement in the country, first with his books, then the short-lived public access show, finally with the consultations. He never moved from the rent-controlled apartment he had inherited from his father, who, wise man, had also put his name on the lease, but the neighborhood had changed around him, and the people he and others had fought so hard to free in years past now became his captors. Sudden gunfire any hour of the day or night. Drunken brick and bottle fights on the stoop or in the stairwell over bottles of wine or cigarettes or a PCP-soaked cigar. Infant crackheads mewling like gutshot cats through the twilight. Predatory hookers who would do anything for $20 or a vial of crack, and wouldn't take no for an answer.

But we went. The movement needed him more than ever.

"One more flight," Rick said.

We were pausing on the fourth floor landing to let three guys with a big-screen television hustle their way downstairs. They didn't look at us and we didn't ask them any questions. Anybody with a tv that big in a neighborhood like this deserved to get ripped off, you ask me. But I didn't applaud them or anything, I just hung there on the landing, listening to see if they made it all the way down with the tv intact. At some point I heard a grunt, then a crash. Elaborate cursing ensued, followed by quick footsteps, a door swinging open, then silence.

The apartment building was like a bad dream in a bad movie about worse people. There were things on the stairs and the landings I refused to believe I was seeing, things I don't want to remember. We heard arias of hatred and despair swirling from behind metal doors dented and scraped and festooned with elaborate and disturbing graffiti.

"Come on," I said, and pushed Rick ahead of me.

Rick and I were co-chairmen of the People's League Against Corporate Welfare. It was a shitty acronym and we were a marginal group, but my grandfather, who used to march with the Master during the 60s, always said that you had to find your own fight and take your stand there. If everyone gravitated to the same cause, he said, The Man would squash us all like roaches. This way, scattered as we were, we were still roaches, but we were impossible to wipe out in one fell swoop. But no one would even bother to take a swipe at us if we didn't make it onto the protest radar, and with a name like PLACW, we were stealth all the way. Safe, but ineffectual.

We reached his door. There was no number, just a mind-numbing mass of bumper stickers pasted one over the other, decade after decade. I pressed my finger against a *Gary Hart '84* and felt it and the others behind it give beneath my finger. It was like touching a holy relic. This door was a living history of the fight against The Man.

Rick stood watch behind me as I tried to knock. It was like punching a stack of tissues. I looked for a buzzer. Nothing. Finally inspiration struck me and I took out two quarters, held them together and wrapped on the brass door knob. Nothing. I kept at it for a good two or three minutes until finally I heard footfalls behind the door. I reached back and touched Rick.

"Okay, man," I said.

I expected a long series of deadbolts to be pulled back, but instead the door slid silently open and I stood face to face with a tall, willowy woman with Indian-straight black hair held in place with a head band. She was beautiful. She was holding a pistol.

"You from PLACW?" she said. She pronounced it "pee lack wuh."

"Yeah. We say PlaceW," I said.

"It's a stupid acronym," she said, and stood back from the door.

I hesitated, but Rick pushed me from behind.

"I don't like it out here," he said.

I stepped across the threshold into a dense cloud of smells that took me back nearly twenty years to when I would visit my grandfather, confined to a wheelchair by then, in his little shack in upstate New York. Patchouli, joss sticks, cheap dope and wine. The place was a mess, piles of books, odd old furniture, discarded stereo equipment and ravaged electronic machinery everywhere. The woman lead us down the hallway to the living room, which looked like the inside of a rat's nest, jam packed with memorabilia from every protest, sit-in, love-in, teach-in and smoke-in of nearly half a century. It was hippie heaven.

I was expecting the woman to call out to him in some back room, but then part of one of the piles of clothes moved and there he was, sitting in a corner on a lazyboy, wrapped in a plaid house robe and wearing fluffy bunny slippers with worn, tattered ears. The Master. He looked like he had put on a little weight since the last picture

I'd seen, when he had been up at Love Canal, exhorting a crowd of dubious-looking protestors. His hair was a faint frizzy halo, ghost of its former near-Afro glory, and the trademark bushy mustache, trimmed now, looked like something a kid had drawn above his lip in eyeliner. But when he spoke, it was the same alarming sound that had galvanized two generations of activists, the sound of a finely-tuned piece of precision machinery with a handful of gravel thrown into it.

"By the hour or by the slogan? Choose your poison!"

There was nowhere to sit, hardly anywhere to move. We stood about fifteen feet away while he meditatively rubbed his upper lip and scowled at us, his bunny slippers, several inches off the ground, twitching as though they were anxious to hop down a hole.

I looked at Rick. He shrugged.

"By the hour?" I said.

"That a question or a statement?" he said.

"By the hour," I said again.

He leaned over and spit into an emptied plastic gallon ice cream container.

"You with Pee Lack Wuh?" he shouted.

"PlaceW," I said.

"Stupidest fucking acronym I ever heard. Almost as bad as WUT."

"Never heard of it."

"Of course you didn't! I told them to change the fucking thing! Women United Together! Sounds like some dumbass southerner asking a question! 'Wut?'" He twisted his face into what must have seemed to him the sneer of an Alabaman confronting the question, what is two plus two. "'Change it!' I said. And they did. And now nobody even remembers WUT. But they sure as hell know NOW!"

I had known that he was responsible for NOW, but not the circumstances under which he had given birth to the name. The other stories were legion. PETA. MADD. And the slogans, too.

When you dug deep enough, you found his fingerprints on "Do Not Bend, Fold, Spindle or Mutilate Me" and "One, Two, Three, Four, We Don't Want Your Fucking War!" and "No Justice, No Peace," and "The People United Will Never Be Defeated." The list went on and on. He was the godfather, or midwife, depending on your metaphorical tastes, to an entire generation of sloganeering, of posters and placards and bumper stickers. The man's fertile brain had dreamed its way into the lexicon of protest and civil disobedience the world over. He should have had his crooked, scowling face on Mt. Rushmore, or on the new $20 bill.

"Place-W," he laughed sadly. He shook his head and placed a hand against his face. "God help us. Give me the details again."

I explained to him our nascent movement. No hippies, no pot smokers, no easily marginalized counterculturalists, but a serious organization of serious people. Accountants and bookkeepers, the keepers of the tills, the guardians at the gate. We were the number crunchers unappreciated by the vast majority of Americans, and yet we were the ones who understood the peril all around us, the mounting debt, the deficits, the spending, the slick slope of insolvency ahead, and amidst it all, slack-hipped whores in Washington spreading wide for every corporate contributor, writing legislation that created tax loopholes, funded obscene incentives, manipulated depreciation allowances and expenditures and write-offs, provided for off-shore havens and out-sourcing that were enlarging the coffers of the few and driving the country to hell in a hand basket. Well, I told him most of that.

"And Pee-Lack Wuh is the best you could come up with?" he said. "What do you guys intend on putting on your posters? 'Don't B Bad?'"

Rick nervously shuffled his feet.

"We were thinking about 'Corporate Responsibility, It's the Right Thing to Do'. "

The Master laughed or coughed or both. The result was another splotch into the bucket at his side. He wiped his mouth.

"Give me a pillow, I'm going to sleep," he said.

I started looking for a pillow.

"I was joking, for crying out loud! *Give me a pillow: you're boring me?* Is this what looking at numbers all day does for you?"

I said "no," and Rick said "yes," simultaneously. The Master shook his head.

"Listen," he said, shifting his weight on the lazyboy. "Civil Disobedience, Public Protest, Activism, whatever you want to call it, is showbiz and marketing. You got that? It's not about changing the attitudes or the minds or the behaviors of the people you're picketing, because they don't give a shit and they'd just as soon run you down in the streets with a tank like the commies did in Tianamen Square as look at your pathetic cardboard and tempera sign."

I'm not normally a sensitive guy, but feeling as I did that we were really stepping out on this issue, putting our careers and reputations on the line, I wanted to be treated with a little more respect. I snorted.

"The camera," he said, then coughed. "The *camera*. The *camera* is the audience. The *camera* is the point. You got to reach the fucking *potatoes* at home. The moldy couch potatoes with eyes growing all over them. Ha! You like that image? They got green mold and they're soft and they got these milky flaccid eyes growing on them. *They* are the ones. It's all about *them*. The others, the people who write the checks or go down to City Hall and join the singing or the chanting, they're not who you're after, because they're already figured into the equation. You have to change the equation, and the way you do that is by changing the potatoes! And how do you change the potatoes?"

He cocked his head toward us as though he expected to hear us thinking. I was coming up with blanks.

"You supplant the crap that's already in their heads. You put your slogan where the newest Dodge commercial used to be. You get them where they live. You rile them up. You get *them* on the streets."

I saw six-foot tubers shuffling down Constitution Avenue, pendulous pale eyes jiggling.

"But to do that," the Master said, "you have to start off with a name that's memorable, then you have to have at least one slogan that's going to help you slay the dragon."

"So what's our name?" Rick said.

The Master shouted to the back of the apartment. "Sally!"

The woman appeared, a paperback Micky Spillane in one hand and the pistol still in the other.

"Yeah?" she said.

"Time's up." He turned to us. "You come back in two days."

"Okay," I said. "Good. Two days. What—what do we owe you?"

He pulled back the sleeve of his house robe and looked at a narrow wrist watch. His lips moved silently, then he let the sleeve slide back down and looked up at us.

"Bring me a television. 32 inch screen. In the box."

"A TV?" I said.

Sally motioned toward the door with the pistol.

"You heard the Master," she said. "Now it's time to go."

The PLACW office was a separate phone line, an answering machine, a website and e-mail address. Membership numbered about 150, but that, in some cases, I suspected, included spouses and children. But that was okay. This was an issue that affected all of us, and the sooner more people realized that and got their wives or husbands and kids involved, the sooner we would have a sane corporate environment in this nation. And that would turn the country around.

I, of course, was the President. Rick was Executive Vice-

President. We both worked for the same mid-sized accounting firm, which will remain unnamed for obvious reasons.

I began feeling self conscious answering the phone, "Place-W. This is the President speaking. How can we change America?" I almost said, "Pee-Lack-Wuh," several times. It was part embarrassment, part acknowledgment that we were in a state of flux, about to undergo a fundamental and evolutionary transformation. We were going to be imminently and irrevocably changed. Naming is making, I learned in a linguistics class in college. We were about to be made.

But in the meantime, before Tuesday, there was business, however slight, to attend to. The World Corporate Alliance was meeting in D.C. in three weeks, and we had been invited to be part of the protest. Things were going to be far more orderly than they were last year, with assigned places for organizations in the "parade route," as the city officials had declared it. It was a protest, not a parade, but you had to get a parade, not a protest, permit. Language. Semantics.

And we had to organize our own people, which is harder than you might think, as most of us are accountants, and are, by nature, retiring people. The last thing an accountant wants is to have his picture plastered on the front page of *The Washington Post* getting his ass kicked by a mounted policeman.

But through it all I couldn't get the excitement out of my veins. I did my job, I answered the Place-W phone, and I surfed the net, looking for information about The Master. I felt that somehow I might be able to get into his head and anticipate what he was cooking up for us. Maybe, you know, save us a few bucks.

I Googled him and came up with 697,014 hits. We had just finished our quarterly reports, so we had some time on our hands. I followed the arc of his career, learned the things I had heard suggested or relearned the things I already knew: He gave Lennon "Give Peace a Chance"; rumor had it that Dr. King gave him a draft of the "I Have A Dream" speech to "pep it up"; "My Body, My Choice": his baby. But there was something else, too, rumors more than anything else, but still disturbing: there were suggestions he was playing both sides of the street. He happens to vacation in Bermuda the same week as a prominent evangelist, and two weeks later "It's a Child, Not a Choice" appears on the first bumper sticker in Ventura County. "You can have my gun when you pry it from my cold, dead fingers," first appears in a brochure not long after he makes a visit to a nephew in Fairfax County, national headquarters for the NRA. "It's Morning Again in America." And on and on.

I didn't want to believe it, but the thread of circumstantial evidence was sufficient for a reasonable person to entertain the unreasonable: the man was just in it for the money.

Tuesday approached. We bought a TV at one of those electronics superstores. Looking at the various slogans—"Just Because" a new one enjoined—I couldn't help but wonder if the Master had had his hand in that, too.

"Sony or Mitsubishi?" Rick asked.

"Which one is lighter?" I said.

"Sony, no baloney," The Master said.

Rick and I stood panting in the only available space in the living room, dripping sweat onto the cardboard box.

"You want us to take it out of the box?" I asked.

He shook his head.

"Someone's coming for it in a couple of days."

"Okay."

He stared at us, then vigorously scratched his head.

"It's got front panel inputs, digital filtering," Rick said.

"That's wonderful."

Silence. In the back of the apartment I heard Sally talking in terse tones to someone on the telephone.

The Master looked off into the distance.

"The world doesn't make sense to me anymore. Everything is too—too fluid. You don't know where you stand. I saw a Natural Resources Defense Council bumper sticker on a Hummer the other day. What the fuck is that, I ask you? What next? Exxon sponsors a water park?"

Rick laughed and the old man shot him a scalding look.

"It's hard to know what's what anymore," I said.

"Bobby Dylan said it years ago, but I didn't want to believe him," he said. He stared through me. "Socio-osmotic politics."

Rick started scratching at his neck.

"What's our name?" he said.

"This isn't like naming a puppy," The Master said. "This is serious shit. This can make or break you. You give a puppy the wrong name, it's quirky or shows personality or it's cute. There's nothing cute about accountants on a crusade." He said the word "accountants" as though he were trying to cough a piece of popcorn up from his throat.

I shrugged.

"So I got you three."

"Three?"

"Three. Accountants For Truth and Economic Reform: AFTER. National Organization of Accounting Honesty: NOAH. And Sane Accounting for a New Economy: SANE."

They all seemed too obvious now that he mentioned them, but we had been kicking names around for a year and hadn't even come close. PLACW was we had come up with.

"You *are* The Master," I said.

He shrugged, made a face that was half sour, half self congratulatory.

"What about slogans?" Rick said. "We've got the World Corporate Alliance coming up."

The Master turned from us and shuffled to his lazyboy. He

leaned over and hawked a lunger into the bucket.

"It'll be a surprise," he said. "I'll bring them to the march."

I wanted to call *The Post* and give them a scoop: The Master was coming out of seclusion to march again. But Rick talked me out of it. What if he didn't show? I'd lose my credibility with the one reporter at *The Post* I knew, whom I had been trying to get to take PLACW seriously for over a year now. No need to endanger that situation. I had to look past the wow factor to the long term. He wouldn't even let me tell other members of the organization.

"Think of all the ways word can get turned around and then leaked," he said. "If you only tell ten people, thousands will know by this weekend, and they'll all have the wrong story."

Rick was right. I tamped down my enthusiasm, bit my tongue and pretended that all was normal as I watched the city agitate itself toward the weekend's climactic struggle.

The World Corporate Alliance came to D.C. every year in the spring, and every year there was a counter-culture protest of epic proportions. Buses arrived from the four corners of the continent bearing Mexican campesinos, Guatemalan banana plantation workers, Inuits from the Arctic, Down Easters, Pacific Northwest Ecowarriors. Ancient Euro-vans, micro-buses and hybrids clogged the Beltway from all points on the compass, packed full of aging hippies, radicalized Soccer Moms, disaffected Gen Xers, alternative energy activists and guys like us, number crunchers who saw the writing on the wall and knew that something had to change.

My girlfriend, Lacy, was apolitical, although she said she "admired my enthusiasm and daring." She had grown up inside the Beltway, the daughter of an Agriculture Department administrator who had never even seen a farm. "It's better that way, Dad says. He's completely objective. He doesn't even know what dirt smells like." The lesson she had learned from her father was that politics didn't really matter. The bureaucrats ran everything, and no one elected them. She would listen to my carefully reasoned arguments about the debt and corporate malfeasance and government shirking of fiscal responsibility, usually on Sunday mornings as we rested in bed and shared sections of *The Post*, but mostly she was just humoring me. "You're so cute when you're apoplectic," she said once, giving me a hug after I had declaimed about Third World Debt Relief for twenty minutes. "We've nearly ruined Argentina!" was the line I think most impressed her. She made me make love to her again right then and there.

I basically had to lie to other members of the group, though, when they asked me about slogans for the march. I had told them of our new name at the weekly meeting—SANE—and everyone was excited, mustering the kind of raw energy accountants only muster at the word "audit." People wanted to break out the brushes and butcher paper right away and start painting, but I prevailed upon them to wait. Slogans were being prepared for us, I told them, and it would be well worth the wait. Grudgingly, they accepted my admonitions to be patient.

At night I had disturbing dreams. In one, The Master was late for the march, and so I went to his apartment to look for him. A gunfight was blazing between two women holding babies and firing at each other up and down the stairwell from different floors. I pressed myself to the wall and ascended. When I got to his door, the bumper stickers were all now in foreign languages, mostly Asian with non-western alphabets. The swooping, elegant characters and symbols detached themselves from the surface of the door and enmeshed me like a giant spider web. I fought my way through the alphabetic arabesque into the apartment, and as soon as I broke the plane of the threshold, I was in a place I didn't recognize, a gleaming, white expansive space, high ceilings, white oak hardwood floors, opened windows through which warm scented breezes blew. I wandered through more square footage than I thought was allowable by law for a mid-town apartment, seeing no one, hearing no one. When

I finally found The Master, he was standing in the farthest room, a place with twenty foot high ceilings. Against the white wall, a white canvas, nearly its equal in size, had been secured by bolts. The Master stood, chin resting on his fist, considering the wall. I looked, saw nothing, then looked at him. His eyes were fixed on the canvas, unblinking. I looked again and saw, dead center in the canvas, a figure in white, an actual moving entity, a whiter white than the canvas, a three-dimensional rendering, a tiny human being. Leaning closer, I saw the person was me, but a barely recognizable me—bald, large-headed, hairy chested. I was writhing and twisting my arms into impossible figures, and my mouth was moving soundlessly, wordlessly. I turned back to The Master and he smiled a knowing smile, as if to say, "See?"

In another, I was at the supermarket looking for fresh lamb, a meat I never eat, when I heard a commotion on the other side of the store and investigated, finding The Master standing at one of those demonstration desks where women, usually attractive, are offering samples of chicken salad or trail mix in little paper cups. But he was doing a puppet show with a cucumber and a tomato. People were laughing like crazy, but I didn't see the humor in what he was doing: positioning the tomato at one end of his table and then approaching it with the cucumber, which moved in sidewinding fashion, snakelike, until it got close enough to pounce on the tomato. A fierce fight would ensue, with the cucumber finally smashing the tomato to fleshy pieces. Then he would repeat it. His audience howled and made lewd remarks about the tomato.

The day of the protest arrived. I had had a sleepless night, tossing so much that Lacy kicked me out of bed and made me sleep, if you could call it that, on the living room futon. I would drift off somewhere, then snap back into fretting wakefulness with some random image, mindtrash from the day gone by, apprehension over the day ahead. I saw The Master's face, free floating in the space behind my eyelids, eyes blazing as he denounced some element of runaway corporate hegemony, the spit flying as he excoriated Wal-Mart and CitiBank and Exxon and other poster children of corporate excess. And he will be there for us today, I remember telling myself in my semi-conscious state. There for us.

The protest kicked off at 10 sharp. There were eighty-six groups represented. We were number eighty-four, in front of Children Against Ugliness and Lies, and Plumbers League United for Nurturing a Greater Economy. Befitting our image, we were the only group in suit and tie. We took our fair share of odd looks and whispers. Distrust registered on each face that appraised us, and it was hard not being able to identify and defend ourselves. But we had no placards, no signs, no slogans. We were SANE, but we were anonymous. Several times credential checkers approached us and I had to produce our parade credentials. "You guys really ought to get a sign," one of them said. "Our sign is coming," I said. "You'll see."

Or maybe not. Because ten o'clock rolled around and from the front of the protest route, nearly two miles long, we heard, rolling back to us in waves, the whistles, airhorns and shouts announcing the beginning of the march. Someone in the group ahead of us—BLANCHE was their acronym, but I couldn't get anyone to tell me what it meant—had an iPad streaming CNN, and could tell us what was happening at the head of the route. "We're moving forward!" they shouted back to us, and we passed word back to CAUL and PLUNGE. But then nothing happened for ten minutes, until finally, with a lurch, the heads in front of us surged forward.

The parade route would take us down 14th, blocks from the White House and the Capitol, but right in front of the hotel where the WCA was meeting. The networks would be there—they always were for this protest, one of the oldest and largest in the capitol—and the print journalists were sprinkled among the protestors. Some of the smaller cable outfits had camera crews interspersed among us, asking the same, inane questions they asked at every protest:

"What are you hoping to accomplish today?" (I heard one college-aged kid ahead of me say, with gusto, "Get laid!") "Do you really think that protests make a difference to those in power?" "How many times have you been involved in protests?" I was waiting for someone to interview me. I had studied these protests over the years, the coverage, and I knew what to avoid if approached by a reporter, what to say so that I didn't sound like an obvious whackjob commie wiccan radical loser. I would avoid cliches and sloganeering, abstractions and the quotation of the standard protest authority figures. I would be precise, sincere, and professional. I had practiced a twenty-second sound bite that could easily be snipped at fifteen, ten or five seconds as well. I would say, "The average American citizen needs to know that large corporations in this country enjoy tremendous, unfair and unethical advantages through the collusion of a corrupt and paid-for Congress, which puts the interests of millionaires and billionaires ahead of working families, and helps corrode the fabric of trust that makes this nation great." Not radical, not screetchy, not preachy, not clueless. Articulate, impassioned, reasonable, composed. It was a long shot, but I also bought lottery tickets once a week. When opportunity knocked, you had to be ready to open the door.

We started moving. Rick nudged me.

"Where is he?" he asked.

"He'll be here," I said. "He told me he'd be here."

We marched. The sun came out and the humidity rose. Others were comfortable in their saffron robes, shorts and sleeveless t-shirts. In our suits, we roasted. I felt myself plastered with sweat. Around us, chants, slogans, songs filled the air. We were silent. I marched scanning the onlookers, most of whom were police and press. He owed us slogans. We had bought him a television.

My people began to grumble. We were heckled by onlookers. "Hey, look at the suits!" "Who are the suits?" "What's with the suits, Suits?" "Agent provocateurs!" Rick said he wanted to hurt somebody, and it was even money that the somebody was me. I grew angrier with each trudging step. Because we looked different, because we weren't readily readable, suddenly we were the issue, and not the rapacious behavior of the corporations we knew were engaged in deceit, lies and illegal behavior. Here we were, out in the open, putting our jobs on the line, and being treated like gutter scum for it!

We soldiered on, helicopters overhead like malignant flies. "La Mosca, La Mosca!" we heard the Guatemalans cry. At each closed-off intersection, sawhorses blocked the street and police cruisers sat purring, their blue lights spinning lazily like carousel strobes. Enterprising camera crews had set up scaffolds at strategic points—the Labor Department, for one—so they could shoot down at the marchers and get a different perspective than competitors.

And it seemed that word preceded us. People were on the lookout for the marching suits without a slogan or a sign to their name. I could hear people calling up ahead now: "Where are the suits? Are the suits coming yet?"

We approached the hotel. We'd been marching for nearly two hours. The last time I turned to do a status check, it looked like nearly half of SANE had bugged out. I didn't mind that people had left, but it was how they were leaving, sneaking off, basically, that galled me. We were about integrity, not self, not ego, not worrying about being embarrassed.

I was discouraged and physically drained when we finally reached the hotel. The Master. The Bastard. We had lugged that fucking television up four flights of stairs in the worst neighborhood in the city. We took our lives in our hands to get him his Sony WEGA, and this was our reward?

And there was the hotel. This towering edifice of greedhead indulgence, a place that charged ridiculous rates because guests would deduct the costs as business expenses, and you and I would end up paying for it, not IBM or Norfolk Southern or United or

SYSCO. If only a reporter would question me now! I could make my statement and point to the hotel and say, "See! That's the problem right there! It's as plain as day!"

And then I saw him. He was there after all, there in the hotel, looking out of a second story window right over the road. He stared down at the protest march, standing next to the CEO of Globatron. They were having an animated discussion, from the looks of it. Then the bastard saw me and waved. He waved!

I just stopped and everybody stopped behind me. We were the tail end of the parade, sure, but the two groups behind us numbered in the hundreds. A confused murmur rose from the ranks.

"There! There he is!" I yelled. And a second later, other SANERs shouted the same thing. "There! There he is!" That became our impromptu, half-assed slogan.

I pointed at him and he pointed back, smiling, giving me the thumbs up. I turned to Rick.

"Do you see him? Do you see?"

"Do you see him?" someone yelled behind me.

"Who?" Rick said. He squinted into the sun.

"HIM!" I said, and made him follow my pointing finger. "There he is! There he is!" And then, and I still don't know why I said it, I yelled, "Get him!"

They kept me in the hospital for two days to make sure I didn't have any permanent brain damage. The swelling had gone down by then, but the wicked purple wound with its insect-looking sutures was pretty impressive. They gave me some pain killers and told me not to wash my hair for another week.

No one knows how I got hurt. One minute I was at the front of the crowd pressing toward the hotel, the next I was cowering and screaming in pain as the surge of people stepped all over me. I had the waffle print of industrial strength sandals on my shoulder for a week and a curious set of bruises that permanently discolored my thighs.

They made it only halfway across the sidewalk. What, to my suddenly inspired imagination, should have been a tidal wave of righteous rage crashing upon this icon of corporate hubris, ended up, instead, no more than a feeble lapping of indolent waves upon the arrival apron of the Excalibur, as if some standing water had been splashed out of a gutter by a passing SUV. Police and private security mopped them up in a matter of minutes and loaded the paddy wagons for the trip to the detainment facility.

I was bleeding enough so that they took me directly to the hospital, where, while I was being sewn up by a nervous resident, I was charged with creating a public nuisance and ordered to appear in court the next week. I did, pleaded guilty on the advice of counsel, and paid a $100 fine.

SANE wavered, almost broke, but recouped, reconstituted and continued, albeit without me. My leadership was woefully deficient during the protest, Rick explained during the executive board meeting where I was ousted, putting the entire membership at risk, and since I had been fired for my apparent incitement of the "riot," I was no longer eligible for membership, which was limited to "professionals working in the field for at least one full year prior to application."

"Maybe when things settle down a little bit," he explained. "You know, you get resettled, get back to work, we let things blow over for a while. I mean, everyone's thankful for the name, but people got hurt out there."

The vote was unanimous, 6-0. They gave me a pro-rated refund of my membership dues and let me keep my Hotmail account for another six months. I wanted to leave them with a few choice, bitter comments, but when I opened my mouth to speak, all I could say was, "Whatever."

I was on my way home from the meeting where I was exiled from the organization I helped found when I realized I was only a few dozen blocks away from The Master's apartment. Maybe it was the pain killers. I don't know. But I found myself driving down his street, looking for the landmarks we had used last time—the liquor stores on four adjacent corners, the burned out church across the street.

A moving van was parked out front of his building. Two guys were carrying a sofa down the front steps when I arrived. They didn't acknowledge me as they hefted the piece of furniture into the back of the van.

"Well, shit, then," one said to the other, "train me how to use the machine, you know what I'm saying?"

"All right," the second man said.

I mounted the steps on unsteady legs. Going up the stairwell, I tried to think of something to say to the man who had let me down after lifting my hopes so high. Several pithy comments occurred to me, but what I settled on when I reached the fourth floor landing and turned down the hallway was a simple, "Fuck you!"

Except I was too shocked to say anything when I reached his door, or, I should say, his doorway. The door itself was gone. Inside the apartment, several people were boxing things up, moving furniture around, cleaning up with broom and mop. When I entered, no one paid me any attention. The place was being cleaned out. The living room was nearly empty, and along the four walls white rectangles bore witness to posters and paintings that had hung there for decades.

"What's going on?" I asked no one in particular.

No one answered, but I did hear the familiar voice from the back of the apartment.

I found him in a large room full of filing cabinets, almost unrecognizable in a yellow jumpsuit and Yankees ball cap. Sally, pistol holstered on her thigh, was writing something down on her clipboard. The Master interrupted what he was telling her when he saw me.

"You!" he said. "You're quite the feisty one!"

"Fuck you!" I said.

Sally looked up from her clipboard and I immediately regretted cursing the old man. He smiled at me.

"Remember, he who curses first, loses," he said. "I think it's Ben Franklin, but I'm not sure."

"You betrayed us. You left us out to dry."

He shrugged. "It was unfortunate."

"And then you went to the hotel! You were with *them*. Them! I heard that you had gone over to the other side, but—"

"My cousin," he said. "The Globatron CEO is my cousin Mort from Dayton. We were meeting for lunch."

I was flabbergasted.

"Besides," he continued. "I'm not on sides any longer. I'm retired!"

"What? Retired? How can you retire from, from fighting for what is right? From fighting for the weak and the downtrodden against the, against the—the—the predations of the mighty and the wealthy?"

"My Uncle left me his condo in Daytona Beach," he said, his voice an odd mixture of fatigue and sunshine. "I'm old. I'm tired. I want to learn how to fish."

I wanted to smack the Yankees hat off his bald head and give him a wedgie through his jumpsuit, to give him some of the medicine I had been force fed at the Excalibur. But there was Sally.

"People believe in you," I said. "They depend on you."

"They need to believe in themselves. Some old Emersonian self-reliance. Look at you—you took matters into your own hands that day. You led the charge!"

"I got my ass kicked!"

"And you're stronger for it, I'll bet you! Ah, hell," he said, waving his hand dismissively, "we all got our asses kicked in the 60s. Why, if you didn't take a beat down from the Man, you were nothing. Civil Rights, Anti-War, we got the shit kicked out of us from dawn to dusk and at midnight, too. And we liked it! It was our badge of honor!"

My head was throbbing. I leaned against a filing cabinet, took out my bottle of painkillers and dry-swallowed a couple Vicodin. The Master snorted.

"At least you got some painkillers! Back in the day it was ThunderBird and maryjane, which will do you in a pinch, but it ain't quite up to snuff with quality pharmaceuticals. We could have moved mountains if we had the kind of meds you kids got these days."

I willed spit into my parched mouth and swallowed to clear the pills.

"You never gave us our slogans," I said. "Our signs. Our banners. We were naked out there. Why?"

He took off his baseball cap, carefully rounded the bill, looked at it meditatively. A quick motion to Sally, a simple nod of his head, and she was gone, but not without first pointing a finger at me, and then at the grip of her pistol. Soon we were alone in silence.

"Well," he said. "What can I tell you?" He looked down at the hat in his hand, smiled like a guilty schoolboy and shrugged. "I couldn't come up with anything to say!"

I gripped the bannister for support on the way down the stairs, my knees turned to liquid, but it was more what I had heard than what was in my bloodstream that had me staggered. The Master, stumped. The legendary river of words run dry. Outside, the waning sunshine had turned the street a pulsing, living orange. Traffic oozed by. I looked for signs of the apocalypse.

I couldn't remember where I had parked my car, so I just turned and started walking. Billboards lining the street ahead mocked me with catchy phrases and memorable slogans. I was implored to be and do and buy and ride and drink and sell and fly and screw. I averted my eyes and marched.

sPAWNing

Chris' mother woke him up at five in the morning and told him to pack some clothes.

"Hurry up and put your things in the Jeep," she said.

"Where are we going?" he asked groggily.

"Just pack your things and put them in the car."

They took the Jeep Cherokee and left the house in Upper Michigan hours before first light. A strong wind drove the rain into the windshield until they reached the Mackinac Bridge. Once or twice they hit patches of sleet that hissed and clicked on the roof. Chris felt nervous about his mother driving in the dark because her eyes were still swollen, but she told him to get some sleep, so he crawled in the back seat and made a pillow from his sleeping bag. The worn shocks made for a gently swaying ride and before he could think very much about the trip ahead he was asleep.

They made their first stop at a gas station in Saginaw. Chris sat up when he sensed that they had stopped moving and saw the attendant cleaning the windshield. Over the sound of the interstate he heard the pinging of the gas pump as it ticked off the gallons

Kurt Jose Ayau

and dollars. His mother came out of the convenience store and paid the attendant when he had finished filling the tank. He noticed she had put her sunglasses on. She climbed in behind the wheel and pushed her heavy coat onto the seat next to her. When she turned to look at him, he saw two small reflections of himself in the mirrored lenses.

"Hungry?" she said.

"A little bit."

"Chew on this. We'll stop for lunch in Flint."

She handed him a strip of beef jerky and started the Jeep. He crawled back into the front seat and took a bite of the meat.

"I wish I was old enough to drive," he said.

"So do I."

They spent the night in Bedford, Pennsylvania, in a long, narrow motel overlooking the Pennsylvania Turnpike. On a row of trees across the parking lot faint green leaves shivered in the dim streetlights. The leaves were small and translucent. When he lay down on his bed he still felt the movement of the car and heard the trucks on the interstate downshifting as they approached the tollbooth a half mile away. He couldn't sleep. Finally he pulled a chair up to the window and watched the trees. Their tender leaves shook aimlessly in the wind. Up in Michigan the trees were still bare and when the wind blew, their naked branches stretched like grasping claws.

Chris looked at his mother. She had turned away from him in her bed. He was glad that with the glasses and the way she wore her hair, no one on the trip so far could tell that she had two black eyes. He didn't know if it was good or bad that her eyes were hidden. She was pretty and men were always saying things to her. Now on the trip the guys in the restaurants and gas stations were acting very friendly. He thought that maybe if these men could see the black eyes they would leave her alone. But no: they might feel sorry for

her and want to help out, and that probably wouldn't be good. He didn't like it when men were too friendly with her. Neither did his father. It caused problems between them that sometimes led to the fighting.

When he finally felt tired he went back to bed. His mother sighed and turned over. He saw her face and it made him feel ashamed.

Each mile seemed to take them deeper into spring. In Maryland most of the trees showed more green. There were flowers growing on the side of the road, and when they stopped at a gas station the trashcan near the pumps was buzzing with flies and wasps. Then finally they got to Virginia, where everything looked lush and green, as though they had driven into a huge terrarium. The air felt heavier to him when he held his hand out the window and made it dive and rise in the rushing wind. Humidity, his mother explained. The word itself sounded heavy in the muggy air.

Last year his mother's parents had retired and moved out into the country about three hours south of Washington, near Charlottesville, where his mother had gone to college. Neither he nor his mother had seen the new house. All they knew about the place was that it had only a wood stove for heat and that it was built right on a pond.

His mother realized that they had missed the driveway when they entered a stretch of ramshackle homes where black people lived. Chris had never seen many black people except on trips to Lansing or Detroit, and certainly not black people in the country. He felt himself staring as they sailed past the box-like houses going one way, and then again as they retraced their path looking for the cottage. At one house two boys about his age seemed to be arguing over a bike. They looked up and stared as the Cherokee drove past. He waved to them and one of them, the shorter of the two, waved back.

They saw the mailbox this time and turned down the drive. The gravel road cut through a field already going wild with weeds and thistles. He rolled down the window when his mother turned off the air conditioning and leaned into the warm wind. Back home patches of snow and ice still lay in gullies on the sides of the road and in the shade. A snowman he had built back in February with some other kids in the sixth grade crouched in a corner of the schoolyard that never got any direct sun, a crumbled remnant of itself. Someone bet it would stay there until June. Where would *he* be in June, he wondered? Where would he be next week? There were still two months of school left. He didn't mind school all that much, but nonetheless he hadn't said anything to his mother. Maybe he wouldn't have to go back to school until September.

The road climbed a small hill, and when they reached the top they saw the pond below them. The forest green cottage was perched on the left side of the water, half of it on stilts, the other half firmly anchored in the ground. There were no trees by the pond. The water shone silver in the sun in irregular patterns marked by patches of pale green lily pads and black algae. Up from the house about thirty yards was a small boat tied to a little dock, and a quarter of the way around the pond from this dock there was another, longer one that reached forty feet into the water.

"Papa never liked your father much," his mother said.

"I know."

"So if he says anything, you just keep your mouth shut."

"I won't say anything."

"You just let him say what he has to say, and that's it."

"Yes."

The front door of the cottage opened and he saw the shapes of his grandparents come out on the deck that ran around the house on three sides. His grandmother waved and started toward the end of the drive where their two cars were parked, but his grandfather stayed near the house with his hands in his pockets.

A jumble of past summers came back to him when he got out of the

car and his grandmother hugged him, enveloping him in the faint familiar aroma of honeysuckle he remembered. He remembered visits in Washington and sleeping with his cousins in the living room, day trips out to the battlefields at Antietam and Bull Run and Gettysburg, walking through the Smithsonian, the Capitol Building. His grandmother told him he'd soon be as tall as his grandfather and then turned to hug his mother.

His grandfather looked at him as though he were a new specimen of some sort and then shook his hand and asked him how he was getting along. He answered, "Fine," and his grandfather said that that was good.

"Did you bring your fishing pole with you?"

"No, sir."

He didn't have a fishing pole, but he didn't think he should admit that to his grandfather. His father had promised to buy him one for Christmas, but instead bought him a bowling ball. When his mother looked at the box the ball came in, she saw that it was much too heavy for him, that it was meant for an adult. The ball was still in its box in his closet.

"That's all right," his grandfather said. "I've got plenty to spare. Why don't you go around the back and take a look at the pond. I'm going to say hello to your mother."

"Sure."

He climbed the stairs to the deck and followed it around to the back of the house where a set of steps led down to the water. He didn't see any fish near the steps, so he went back up on the deck and followed it to the far end of the house where there was another set of steps leading down to the grass at the water's edge. The aluminum boat was beached halfway on land and was tethered to the small dock. He didn't like being on the water very much since he wasn't a good swimmer, but if his grandfather would go with him, he would like to try the boat.

Beyond the dock he saw a strange fluttering just below the surface near land. He caught his breath. He stood still and shielded his eyes from the glare of the sun off the water. It was a rhythmic movement back and forth, a sweeping tail fin. The fish was less than two feet from shore, partially hidden under a canopy of floating algae. He couldn't tell how large it was. Beneath it lay a clear, almost golden, patch of sand. Chris moved forward to get a closer look at it, but at his first step the tail fin lashed out powerfully and the fish was gone in a swirl of sand. He finally let out his breath.

He stepped back from the edge of the water and waited, hoping to see the fish return. Minutes passed and no fish. He moved farther along the edge of the pond, looking for others. Twice more he found the same scene: a cleared out patch of sand with a fish nearby, waiting, waiting. They should be easy to catch, he thought, so close to land, so easy to see. When his grandmother called him in to lunch, he ran hard from the far side of the pond with his pulse strong in his ears, scaring mayflies up from the grass in clouds that fluttered and tumbled in his wake.

But he didn't fish that day. After lunch they unloaded the Cherokee and he and his mother got set up in their rooms. His room was actually part of the front porch, which his grandparents had separated in half with a wall and closed in by putting windows over the screens. There was a small sofa bed and a nightstand in one corner of the room. A couple of bookcases stacked with old hardcover books stood near the door. The dust jackets on the books were faded and torn. An old desk with a lamp and a pencil box on it leaned against the bed. His grandmother showed him how to operate the electric blanket on the bed. It still got a little chilly in the night, she explained.

A series of framed photographs hung from the wall that the porch shared with the house. There were old pictures of Mama and Papa's wedding, of Papa in uniform during World War II, of Chris' mother and her sisters when they were in grade school, of the sisters and their families. There was a picture of him when he was about seven, then a bare patch with a nail showing where a photo had hung, and then a picture of some of his cousins. He looked closely at his mother's picture, thinking that maybe he looked like she did back then. He didn't look much like her now. Maybe there were a few similarities. Maybe the ears, the long neck.

His mother came to his room that night after she and her parents had played cards. He had found a complete set of the *World Book of Knowledge* and was looking through the first volume when she came in holding a glass of clinking ice cubes and stood by one of the windows, looking out at the flitting shapes of moths that battered themselves against the floodlight at the corner of the house. He looked up at her, but she was oblivious to him, so he went back to reading about atolls.

"Do you like it here?" she finally asked.

"It's okay."

She turned to him, and he saw that her eyes looked a lot better. They seemed to have improved since that morning. She would still probably wear sunglasses when they went to town tomorrow, but he felt that if she didn't, no one would pay any attention now to the faint blue half moons beneath them.

"There are those boys down the road who are your age," she said, absently lifting the glass to her lips and drinking. "You could invite them to go fishing."

"Only the small ones are biting. You can't eat them unless you catch a whole bunch of them." .

"Still, it's fun just to do it, isn't it? Isn't that what boys like, just to be out there doing it?"

"I guess."

He felt embarrassed to be listening to her because her words were coming out slurred. He tried to concentrate on a photograph of an atoll being demolished by an atomic bomb test.

"We're going to stay here for a while," she said. "If we go back to Michigan, Daddy won't be there with us anymore. Do you understand?"

"Uh huh."

He brought his face close to the photograph. Tiny palm trees were bent nearly double by the force of the bomb.

"I don't think you understand," she said.

"I do," he said.

He wanted her to leave. He wanted to make her believe him so she would go back to the living room and play cards some more. It was just too much to listen to her.

"Some day you'll understand," she said. "Really understand. There are things you need to know." She finished off her drink. "Don't hold the book so close to your eyes."

She leaned over and rubbed his head kind of hard, and then she left. The smell of the whiskey stayed with him like smoke after she was gone. He pushed the book aside and buried his face in the bedspread and made a sound halfway between a moan and a growl. He had tried not to think about his father all this time, but now it was no good. In his mind he saw his father's face. He was ashamed to see it, but he couldn't help it. It was the face of his father.

The next morning he helped his grandfather mow the lawn. He wasn't particularly keen on doing chores, and at home his mother had to keep after him to do things, but he felt as though he had to please his grandfather. The grass was not very high, but the old man had the mower out there while the grass was still wet with dew. He let Chris push the mower on the second half of the lawn while he rested under the oak tree. Since there was no "yard" to speak of, they could have kept mowing all day. His grandfather arbitrarily set up boundaries and they mowed about half an acre.

Then they started raking up the grass together. They worked toward the middle from opposite ends, Chris dragging his clippings toward large, ambitious piles, while his grandfather arranged a series of neat small hummocks, like way stations on a journey.

At one point Chris looked up and saw movement above the ridge that ran parallel to the road. He followed the three dots until they moved into view on the road heading north. The three dots were three kids, three black kids on bikes. They slowed and stopped as he watched them, and then they seemed to be watching him back. He slowly raised his rake and waved with it. Two of the kids waved back at once, and then the third waved and they started pedaling again.

"Don't pay any attention to the ones in toward shore."

"Why not?"

His grandfather sat in a lawn chair on the deck above him, a paperback book on his lap.

"They're spawning. The females sweep out a spot near shore and lay their eggs and the males fertilize them and keep a watch over them until they hatch. They protect the eggs from blue gills."

"What's that?"

"The small fish you see out there," his grandfather said, pointing out toward a blotch of lily pads. "If you catch the males when they're guarding the nest, the blue gills eat the eggs and pretty soon you don't have any more fish."

"Oh."

He reeled his line in slowly, stepping to the side and maneuvering the twisting night crawler around the spawning nest. He heard his grandmother come out on the deck.

"Not so close, now," his grandfather said sharply.

"What are you scolding him about?" his grandmother asked.

"I don't want him disturbing the spawning nests."

Chris pulled the worm away from the nest, keeping his rod out over the water, until he caught his hook on a lily pad. He pulled and the rod dipped.

"Oh, they won't bite while they're spawning," his grandmother said.

Kurt Jose Ayau

"There's always accidents," his grandfather said, and then, "don't pull so hard. You'll break the line."

He looked up as his grandfather reluctantly set his book on the deck railing and came down the steps to the water's edge. The old man took the rod from his hand and Chris watched as he worked the line back and forth until the hook came free. In the murky green water, he saw a flash of white as the water-logged worm slipped off the hook and sank out of sight.

"Didn't your ... didn't you do any fishing in Michigan?"

"We were supposed to a couple of times, but we didn't," he said.

He seemed to recall one time that the car wouldn't work, or that his father had done something to it. Another time they were all supposed to go out on Lake Michigan with one of his father's friends who had a boat. But when they got to the dock and his mother saw how small the boat was, she refused to get on and wouldn't let Chris go either. His father made them wait in the car while he talked to his friend and then waved from the boat for them to go home without him. On the ride back home Chris felt frustrated about the cancelled trip, but his mother didn't apologize. She didn't say anything. His father came home late and drunk that night without any fish and slammed the door behind him.

"Maybe you should try the dock where there aren't any lily pads. That way you won't lose a worm every time you cast."

"Sure, Papa," he said, taking the rod back.

He picked up the can of worms and started for the dock, feeling small and silly.

That night he found a book of World War II photographs, and sat on the bed thumbing through it. What he was looking for were pictures of planes, the gray, lean shapes of Messerschmidts, P-51s, Zeros. As he flipped the pages looking for dogfights, he heard his mother and his grandparents in the kitchen. They were talking in quick bursts to each other, and though he could hear what they were saying, it wasn't very interesting. People his mother had known in college; friends of his grandparents who had died recently; what had happened to the neighborhood where his mother had grown up.

They began talking in increasingly flat, indistinguishable tones. He lay back on the bed and stared at another photo, counting B-17s in formation over England on their way to Germany, humming to himself to keep the annoying, droning voices in the next room out of his head. He couldn't keep it up, though. He finally stopped humming and listened halfheartedly.

"I'm just thankful he didn't do anything more serious," his grandmother said. "He could have killed you."

His mother said something that he couldn't hear. There was silence for a few seconds.

Then his grandfather said, "Don't know why you waited this long."

He didn't hear his mother's answer. The hot, liquid feeling in his chest made his heart race and he was deaf for a second. He put the book aside and sat up. The sound of their voices had changed, as though they had moved into the living room. He listened hard for a second, then carefully got up from his bed and went to the door. It was opened a crack and he placed his ear against it.

"You could try a separation," his grandmother said. "That's not as drastic."

"Why should she treat the son of a bitch with kid gloves?" his grandfather said. "She's got two black eyes, for God's sake. You want her dead before she does anything?"

"Dad," his mother said.

"Do you want him back? I don't know why you wanted him in the first place. I always knew there was something cowardly about him. A drunkard, a cheat and a wife beater."

He waited for his mother to say something—he wanted her to say something to make him stop—but she was silent. Why was she

Kurt Jose Ayau

letting him say these things about his father? He knew that some of the things might be true, but they didn't have to talk about him this way.

"I always had a feeling," his grandfather said. "Something I just knew. Just the way he looked when he thought you weren't watching him. Sly. Like he was pulling something off all the time."

Chris felt himself making fists and leaned against the door. It squeaked and shut the last inch. He was still holding his breath, wondering if they had heard, when the door jerked open against his shoulder and his grandfather glowered at him.

"It's your bedtime, isn't it?" he asked after a few seconds.

Chris didn't answer.

"Go ahead and get in the shower first."

He moved past his grandfather into the kitchen, his face warm with embarrassment and anger. When he passed his mother he didn't look down at her, even when she reached and touched his arm.

He could feel the slight weight of the worm and the sinker through the line as it writhed on the hook. He had slid the hook through several times, winding the pliant flesh around the barb, and the worm had struggled and excreted a dark grey goo on him. He hated doing it, but when it was over he thought it was a pretty good job. He let the hooked worm swing away from him and pressed the lever forward on the reel, releasing the line.

The bobber and sinker added weight on the line, so the cast went out a good thirty feet and made a double splash on the rippled surface. He reeled the line in a few feet and then stopped, letting the bobber jiggle on the little waves.

Across the water from him he could see that the back door of the cottage was open and he could hear his mother and her father talking. His grandmother had gone into town for lunch with a friend.

Occasional words came across the water to him. "Silly," he

heard, and "predictable " and "telephone," but he didn't care what they were talking about. The words might have something to do with him, but he couldn't do anything about them, so he tried to block them out with the sound of the birds in the cattails, the water, airplanes high above sewing the sky with their contrails.

The wind kept pushing the line toward shore and he kept reeling it in. Suddenly the bobber bounced erratically and disappeared under the water. He pulled the rod back sharply, but there was no weight at the end of the line. He felt a momentary tug, then nothing, as the bobber and the worm came flying out of the water to land at his feet.

He took up the slack in the line and his eyes refocused beyond the bobber on the water. He saw the undulating movement not three feet from shore, a bass hovering over a golden yellow spawning nest. The fish was enormous. He couldn't reckon how long it was, but it made him catch his breath when he saw it. The fish moved in tight circles over the clear sand, stroking its tail like a fan.

He thought about what his grandfather had said about the males protecting the nests, but then his grandmother's words came back, too. "They won't bite while they're spawning." Nothing would happen. But if he did get lucky and caught something, he could just put it back without anyone knowing.

He cast the line out over the bass and slowly reeled it in. The worm twirled as he drew it toward him, a propeller in the water. When the worm reached the fish, he let it drift, gently pulling the line toward the circling gray shape. As it passed directly over the spawning nest, the bass turned and slipped by, barely nudging the hook. He could feel the faintest tug through the line.

He tried jiggling the worm, but the fish showed no further interest, and each jiggle brought the line closer to shore until he had to pull it from the water and cast again. This time he got it farther out so he would have more room and time to play with it. The worm was getting whiter with each cast. Soon he would have to discard it and get another, but that would mean going back to the house. He had left the cup of worms on the deck by the door.

On the fourth cast he pulled the worm over the spawning nest again, but this time faster than before, and he watched the bass strike. The bobber dove a good six inches under the water and he felt the strong pull in the rod. The bass headed for deeper water. The line moved sharply out over the surface of the water as though the fish were drawing with it, using it to mark off boundaries on the little waves.

He yanked back hard and set the hook.

The line went crazy, zig-zagging to the left and then coming back toward him. He reeled in, dropped the tip of his rod toward the water, and reeled and pulled again. The fish came to the surface and exploded out of the pond, its tail swishing as it came up, and then slapping as it reentered the water. He reeled again, holding the butt of the rod against his belly and pulling the tip up hard and quick. The ratchet in the reel began to tick as the weight of the fish became too much to counteract. He started backing away from the water, keeping the tip of the rod up behind his ear. He almost fell once, but he kept his balance and kept backing up. The fish skipped out of the water, fell and thrashed in the tall grass.

He called out for his mother and pulled the fish up the bank away from the pond. It lunged and twisted heavily on the line, its dark gray shape twisting in the deep green grass. Looking at it, he couldn't tell which end was its head. He laid the rod down and held the line loosely in his hand as he followed it to the gasping fish.

The anguished flopping and working of its mouth made something sharp twist inside of him. He watched the gills open and close and felt his own breathing become difficult. He kneeled beside the fish and reached for it, but when it slapped its tail and lifted itself off the ground, he pulled back.

"Mom!"

But she didn't hear him. She and his grandfather were arguing in the kitchen, their voices skipping out to him across the water.

He tried the fish again and this time got a hand on it, but he couldn't hold its slippery body. It quivered and flipped away deeper into the grass. It was as long as a cat's body, and in the brief second that he held it, he could feel its strength and its desperation. But he knew he had to catch it and hold it; he had to take out the hook and put it back in the water.

The second time he touched it, he pressed it down on the grass and got his other hand on its head. The movements of its long body scared him, but he held on and grabbed the line, inching his fingers toward the eyelet on the hook. The fish's mouth popped open and he was surprised at how big and round it was, and the depth of its gullet. The hook was somewhere down in the series of what seemed to be other mouths, each working slowly, opening and closing, as he peered into them. It made him feel sick to reach deep into the fish's mouth, but it had to be done. Once he got the metal between his thumb and forefinger he tried to find the angle of the hook and ease it out, but it didn't budge. He tried pushing in first, then pulling out, then just pulling out. Nothing worked. The hook as stuck fast. The fish's gasping was more pronounced now, and each opening of its mouth lasted longer. It was dying, he knew, and he couldn't help it.

He tried the hook again and felt angry at the fish for not helping him. He saw some blood now on his fingers. At first he thought it was his, but he didn't feel any pain. He reached into the fish's mouth again, then three more times after that. The hook wouldn't give. His chest felt tight, as though a balloon were expanding inside him, threatening to explode. He let the fish fall heavily back onto the ground and went searching through the grass behind him.

He found a fallen limb thick as his wrist. He stripped its branches and snapped it in half by standing on it and pressing it back toward him. Armed with the club, he went back to the fish.

The first blow went wide and hit the thick grass with a swish. He heard from across the water the sound of the kitchen screen door opening, but he didn't pay it any attention. He struck again and the fish jerked as the club hit its side. The third blow fell solidly on the fish's back and sent a shudder through it. Still, he didn't stop. He hit it again. Again. Again.

He had laid down the club and was sitting in the grass when his grandfather ran up to him. The fish was still twitching, but it was just a spasm, the mouth working slowly, now. His grandfather nudged the fish once with the toe of his shoe.

"Why did you kill it?" he asked. "You could have let it go."

He didn't answer. He was trying to keep from crying. The gulping breaths he swallowed burned like water in his lungs.

His grandfather crouched down and picked up the fish by its jaw. The tail shivered tremulously, as though it were cold, while he worked the hook out of its mouth and dropped the line in the grass.

"I guess this is supper," he said.

The old man stood with the fish and looked down at him.

Chris rose up on his haunches and then stood.

"We always eat what we catch," his grandfather said. "I'll show you how to clean it."

His grandfather started back to the house and he nodded and followed him. Halfway there the old man looked down at him.

"What's that on your face?" he asked.

"Huh?"

Chris reached up to his face and felt something dry and circular on his cheek, like a hard tear.

"Scales," his grandfather said.

Chris touched the scale again and felt two more as he moved his hand across his face. He was fascinated by the feel of them under his fingers, as though he were molting into something else and studying the changes. He thought about flicking them off into the pond, but decided instead to wear them into the house for his mother to see.

Calling It off

I hit *Play*.

Blue screen. Static. Then the neighborhood nutjob shuffles by in housecoat and slippers. Left to right, right to left. He disappears down a hallway, reappears, looms Frankenstein-large in the frame, his hair a greasy mess. Sign of the madman, the freak from whom children should run away, run away! He sidles up to the living room window, inserts two fingers between the venetian blinds to sneak a peak at the world outside, where the mail spills from the box at the end of the drive and a month's worth of newspapers dot the lawn like some sick and persistent dog's copious, decomposing turds. He mutters to himself. He shuffles.

It is fresh evidence, taken this morning, and it confirms what I fear.

I hit *Stop*.

This is me? *This*? *Me*? Yes: this: me. How?

People might conjecture: genetics? Life's sometimes sad trajectory? Happenstance? A conspiracy? Simpler than that.

Crazier.

The path from Norman, the stable guy next door ("What's he do again?" people might say. "An accountant? An adjustor?") to the sour-smelling crazy man with all those cats and the station wagon full of empty milk cartons and the yelling about the government and black helicopters and people not making eye contact with you anymore can be a brutally short and straight one. A matter of minor mistakes. You see, I was never the kind of guy who had *goals* for *being*, you know, like the kinds of things the TV "doctors" preach. I didn't have milestones and performance objectives, five-year plans written down in little notebooks. None of that stuff. I just did my thing. *Lived.* Like my father used to say, you get up and have a cup of coffee and figure out what's what, then you go out and do stuff. That was my motto. *Go out and do stuff.* So I did. And I think now that when you live like that, when you're just kind of floating like that, well, you don't have a hold, you don't have a grip. And things can happen. And then things can get out of control. So I guess if you're going to have a motto, you better have a really good one.

They must have a motto, too, some pithy sentiment to motivate them as they start the day, limping and scuffling through the special safety glass doors, feeling their way to their desks. Maybe it's a Helen Steiner Rice poem pinned to their cubicle walls or a Rod McKuen screensaver. Or it could be that they have a banner strung across the entire office, some kind of play on words to do with inspiration and brightness and light bulbs. It's got to be something to do with light bulbs, of course, because that's how they get you, after all. That's how they sucked me in. Those wonderful, last-almost-forever, too-good-to-be-true light bulbs. Special emphasis on the "too-good-to-be-true" part, although not quite in the way you might imagine.

I don't turn the lights on anymore. Instead, I creep in the dark, sometimes shuffling carefully along the wall, sometimes on my knees, sometimes even low-crawling like I'm stretched out under barbed wire with machine gun bullets snapping overhead. Or I use the night-vision function on my camcorder and wade through a wavering sea-green underwater world that's always a half second too slow. I want to believe that nobody knows I'm here. Who would be at home and leave all that shit on his lawn? Who would be at home and never turn the lights on? But I know they're watching. They've been watching for a while.

I don't turn the lights on, because when I start doing that, I'll start burning them out, and when I start burning them out is when they'll try to suck me back in. And they'll work me until they get me, because I am weak, a prisoner of my own kindness.

See, I'm the guy who never says no. I get that from my father, too. I remember the first time I saw him give some money to a beggar on the street. This guy was propped up against a building with a cardboard sign on his lap. He looked grimy and shiny simultaneously, like he had been rolled in the street then shellacked. His sign read: "Public Assestence Needed. Plese Give." He smelled bad. My father dropped a bill in his lap.

"That man can't spell," I said.

"Spelling ain't all it's cracked up to be," my father said.

"But he just sits there," I said. "He doesn't do anything."

"Son, there's no telling why that man is sitting there. We probably don't want to ask him to tell his story. Maybe some hard luck or he drinks too much. I see people like that and I feel sorry for them. So I give him a dollar? So what? I guess I'm just a softie."

When we got home and I told my mother the story, she said, "Yeah, soft in the head." They didn't see eye to eye on the philanthropy thing. They didn't see eye to eye on much. His standard joke: "Of course we don't see eye to eye—she's five inches taller than I am!" Some people say that he was henpecked, and that may be right. I just think that rather than being a weak person, he was extremely kind and steeped in the fine tradition of confrontation avoidance. He never wanted to hurt anyone's feelings.

Kurt Jose Ayau

That's my excuse. That's how it all happened. I've never wanted to be the bad guy, the guy who says "no," the guy who hangs up, the guy who doesn't attend the United Way meeting at work. So I'm the one who buys five boxes of each kind of Girl Scout cookie, who signs up for all the -Thons the neighborhood kids do: Bike-a-Thon, Math-a-Thon, Run-a-Thon, Jump-a-Thon, Slurp-a-Thon, Skate-a-Thon, Kiss-a-Thon, Shrug-a-Thon. I'm the one who sends the poor kids to summer camp in the Adirondacks. I'm the one who helps the American Indians say no to alcohol and yes to self improvement and Casinos. The Kidney Fund, the American Heart Association, the Cancer Society, the Lung people. Eyes, feet, irritable bowel, artificial knees, prostate, kidneys, glaucoma, virulent halitosis, the Inverse Flatulence League—you name it, I got it covered. My cancelled checks are a children's alphabet book of acronyms, a *Gray's Anatomy* chart of bodily causes. DAW, AWH, SJW, ACS, AHS. If there's a body part in need, I'm the man with the cash. They ask, I give. It's part of the stuff I do.

I became such a sure bet that the neighborhood kids didn't even work for it anymore. They came up the walkway and, yeah, they rang the bell and gave me the spiel, but it was like they were doing me a favor now, rushing through the pitch like it was the Gettysburg Address that they had memorized for civics class and they didn't want to appear to be sissies for getting into it *too* much or something. They knew it really didn't matter how they performed, because they knew I always said yes. They could have just held out their hands. And so I learned that there's one thing kindness will get you for sure these days: contempt.

That's the story with the light bulb people, my reward for kindness. They called one day, I said, "Yes," the *relationship* began, and now *this*. (Yeah, a *"relationship"*: that's what they call it. You're not just an anonymous donor to the Disabled Laborers of America, a

faceless name, a nameless face; no, you are an important part of their manufacturing, sales and distribution self-help program.) They told me that the pictures of all Victory Partners (that's what they call you, a *Victory Partner*, V.P. for short) get put up in the factories and warehouses and call centers. You send them a picture with your first check and they scan it and send it around: your smiling face looking down upon the lame and the halt as they labor to make their lives, and our country, better. It kind of weirded me out when they first mentioned it. I saw myself like a Big Brother figure watching them, but then I got his newsletter and I could see all these V.P.s on all these boards and so, you know, it wasn't that big a deal or anything. In fact, it made me feel kind of special. If my father were still alive, it would be the kind of thing he'd appreciate.

I gave to the DLA. And I gave. Of course, they send you stuff. Light bulbs. Trash bags. Air freshener. Window cleaner. Incontinence pads. Carpet de-spotter. But there's only so much of that shit you need, unless you're running an adult day care center or something. My house was filling up with all this stuff; everywhere you looked there was a box with DLA stenciled on it. The other causes, well, in a way it was a blessing that all you got from them was a form at tax time. With the disabled people, they wanted to make you feel like you weren't just *giving* them money, so they sent you this stuff. All this stuff.

It started with a phone call, of course. At least they had the decency to wait until after dinner. I was happily digesting, sleepy, when "Handsome Ed" called for the first time. I never knew if he was, indeed, handsome or not. But he was certainly cheerful. I told him I had never heard of the Disabled Laborers of America before.

"Oh, yeah, Norm," "Handsome Ed" said, "we're the oldest self-sufficient handicapped organization in the country! You know about our light bulbs?"

I didn't know about the light bulbs, so he told me about the light bulbs.

"Wow," I said. "A lifetime guarantee on light bulbs?"

"That's right, sport. If those light bulbs ever, and I mean ever, go out, we'll replace them for the cost of shipping and handling. What you think about them apples?"

What I thought, I can't remember. What I did was order a set of six light bulbs for $50, plus shipping and handling.

"Now, I know you're thinking that $50 is a lot for some light bulbs," "Handsome Ed," said, "but when you figure that the average light bulb costs you $1.29 and lasts for six months, well, you do the math. You're gonna spend $8 for that same bulb over three years, but the $8 you spend on our bulbs is gonna last you forever. And I don't have to tell you how long forever is, do I, pal? And the best thing? You don't have to pay a cent until you receive the bulbs. How about that?"

When "Handsome Ed" spoke it was like listening to a waterfall in the sunlight. You couldn't help but be swept up in his sparkling enthusiasm. I asked him how long it would take for my bulbs to get to me.

"Seven to ten business days, but we can Fed Ex 'em to you if you're sitting there in the dark!" He laughed and I laughed with him. I told him that regular mail would be fine.

"Well, heck, Norm, I've enjoyed fishing with you. Now, I'm going to get my supervisor to give you a call back in about five minutes to verify the order. This is really gonna help us out, pal. So you wait for her call and have a great day!"

With that, he was gone and I was headed down the path of no return.

The light bulbs showed up when promised, I paid my bill, and, I have to tell you, the light bulbs were good. They were great. Bright, clear, and they lasted through the rest of the year while other bulbs I had bought just the week before at the supermarket burned out. When "Handsome Ed" called me back about five months later, I told him I didn't need any more bulbs.

Calling It off

"Course not, Norm! You're set for life with those bulbs, pal. Just remember to keep your packing slip with your order and account numbers. That way, if the bulbs do burn out, (but they're not, kind of like a reverse Catch-22, you know?) you just call us up, give us the numbers, and we set you up again. Got it?"

"Got it."

And I did really think that I had gotten it, that I was done. But "Handsome Ed" had other products to sell, and like clockwork he started selling them to me.

"Hey, Norm," the voice would leap into my head from the earpiece, "it's Handsome Ed!! Time to go fishing, old buddy! How've you been? God's been great to me. I got a great deal on stool softener this month, pal!"

I don't know why "Handsome Ed" always talked about going fishing. I never fished. And we were always talking on the phone. I never had the nerve to ask him just what he meant, though, because he always sounded so upbeat. And, I don't know, something about the way he called me *pal* convinced me he was sincere. He was the first one from ADL to call me. He was how the relationship started. Once he sent me a picture of him in his cubby, and there, over his shoulder, was my picture, watching over him. I felt kind of obligated.

"Handsome Ed" told me about his life, about his kids and his ex-wife, "the tough old lady with the monthly needs." He told me about the problems he had with his neck and the surgery he was facing. I bought a two-year supply of Dura-Strength Heavy Duty Kitchen and Lawn Trash Bags.

"God bless you, pal!" he said. "People are gonna look at you and say, 'Norm? That guy's got it in the bag!' Get it?"

When the others started calling me, I thought "Handsome Ed" had gotten fired, or maybe he quit. The thought occurred to me that his surgery hadn't gone well and that he was now crippled. Maybe they moved him to a new division where he didn't have to sit up at a desk and make phone calls. Then he reappeared again, and when I asked him about the other guys, he played it off like he didn't know what I was talking about.

"What other guys, Norm? Hey, I'm you're only fishing buddy, ain't I?"

"I'm getting these other calls," I said. I had started my notebook then, so I flipped through it and read him some names.

"Never heard of them. I know everybody here. Those aren't our people."

"Whose people are they?" The phone went dead for a few seconds, that kind of empty sound when someone puts you on hold. Then Ed came back, chipper as ever.

"Don't know, pal. I asked the supervisor. She'll get to the bottom of this. In the meantime, how about that stool softener?"

Soon, I don't know how exactly, I was getting calls from coast to coast. It was like "Handsome Ed" had gone into a handicapped restroom and written my name on stalls. "For a quick light bulb sale, call Norman!" "Call Norman—he can't say no!"

Because my phone was ringing all day, every day, from all these handicapped groups with names sounding vaguely similar. Handicapped Laborers of the United States. And American Laborers with Disabilities. And Workers With Challenges. What did I do? I bought. I'm a softie. Soon I was in a "relationship" with "Cherlice" and "Bobby" and "Groender." Eventually, I didn't know who was who, where they were calling from, what exactly they were selling. Or even if I could trust them. I started keeping notes in a little binder I had. The acronyms and the names and the products and the prices just piled up. And when I got confused and couldn't remember who it was I was working with, they all claimed that we had been in a "relationship" for a decade. They all said they had my picture "right here in my cubbie." I was confused. I was lost. And my monthly bill for pricey consumables was burning a hole through my bank account.

So I cut them off. All of them. I didn't mean to at first, I thought I would just scale back, regain my equilibrium, pace myself, but I didn't know who was who anymore, because, heck, there were like a dozen or so, and I swear that some of them started calling with different names. Cherlice became Amanda became Twanda became Nancy. And "Barnacle Bob" was really "Handsome Ed," I'd swear. It was just too much to try and keep it all straight. So I had to make a clean break. There's a term they use in psychology, but I can't remember it anymore. Whatever the term was, it was something I had to do. So I did it. And they got the message, eventually. I was calling it off. I was breaking up with them.

There was a lull, this sweet period when the only time the phone rang it was someone from work asking me about a project or how to get the machines recalibrated. Then it started. First came the calls from the "district supervisors" wanting to confirm my decision, trying to remind me of the *relationship*, all the good I had done, how I had helped pay for children's braces and water heater repairs and overdue rent and a second car so "Cherlice" could take her mother to dialysis instead of accompanying her on the long bus ride with three transfers. I wavered. I paused for long periods of time before answering. I thought of my father and what he would do. Envisioned his smiling face circled by light bulbs and other helpful household products. But that same kind of indiscriminate kindness was why Mom finally left him, was why his path would be the path to disaster, so though I imagined his frowning face, the sour aroma of heartbreak as he sat in his nursing home barcalounger and heard me tell my tale of "no," I knew I couldn't break. I couldn't. I needed my life, and my closet space, back.

There was some stuff still in the pipeline, things I had ordered before I had made my decision. Slowly it all trickled in, and all of it was damaged in some way. Light bulbs were smashed. Boxes full of garbage bags were torn and bags were flapping in the wind on my front porch. I opened a box of air freshener to find the bottle crushed and an oily opalescent scum floating in the shrink-wrapped package. The inescapable, condensed stink of "Mountain Pine" penetrated to the farthest reaches of my house, so strong that it woke me up at night. And everything was accompanied by a packing slip, a bill and a printed card detailing the iron-clad money-back policy. What I should have done was just send all the shit back, but I couldn't even do that. I was paralyzed. If I sent the stuff back and told them it was damaged, they'd probably just send me more. So I decided to just keep the stuff. But, of course, by keeping it all, I owed them money.

That's when they escalated. They were pissed, now, I guess, so they stepped up the pressure. Cars slowed down to a lame man's crawl as they passed my house. My phone rang in the dead hours of the night, but no one was there when I answered. And then somebody burned this weird symbol on my lawn. It looked like a Christmas elf sodomizing a clown. I called the police and I tried to explain who I thought was behind it. The cop taking the report kind of snickered. I thought maybe at first I was just imagining it, but he did it again when I started giving him the names of all the groups I thought might be responsible. I told him I was serious, and then he acted all offended, like I was making some kind of accusation. When he left I knew that nothing was going to happen. He probably didn't even type up the report.

I know it's crazy. I know it's letting things get to me. But by some weird alchemy my generosity became paranoia. I would drive to work and cars would tailgate me, slice in front of me to make a right turn from the left lane, blind me with their high beams, make sudden stops and jagged stunt-driver maneuvers. And from every rearview mirror I'd see the same thing: a handicapped tag dangling

Calling It off

like a taunt. I'd go to lunch and be sitting at the end of the table with a big cup of coffee and a big bowl of soup in front of me and someone—a guy with palsy skittering down the aisle, or a blind woman with an erratic cane flailing like she was dowsing—would smack the table and soup and coffee would slosh and run and dribble into my lap, and I wouldn't get so much as an "excuse me" or "sorry."

Finally, I stopped going out. I called in sick, and then called in sick again. Eventually, Slocum called and told me not to bother coming back. It's okay, because the house is paid for, I have money saved up, and I'm not buying all this junk from the disabled people anymore. I get stuff from the Internet and I can order food from the grocery store, although the last time they delivered it, the guy who brought the bags to my door had a noticeable limp, and he seemed to sneer at me when I gave him what I thought was a pretty good tip. When I unpacked my bags, all of my meat packages had thumb-sized holes poked through the shrink wrap.

I would ask one of the neighbor kids to bring in the newspapers, because once spring comes they'll start killing the lawn, especially all those huge Sunday editions with the special four-color shopping inserts jammed inside, and it will be impossible for anyone to mow it. But the kids have stopped coming. Nobody wants my -Thon money anymore. Maybe word has gotten out. I wouldn't put it past the disabled people. My last phone conversations with them were pretty tense, and there seemed to be the hint of a threat in their comments. I'm pretty sure one of them said, "We'll take you down, bitch," but it could as easily have been, "We'll take down your picture." I was on my cordless in the basement, so I can't be sure.

Now I'm just waiting. Waiting for a pilot with a club foot to crash his plane into my house. Waiting for a delivery driver with a hearing problem to "lose control" of his van, jump the curb, and knife through my living room wall, pinning me beneath my sofa. Maybe it will be a wheelchair ninja cutting my legs out from under me with some deft turns of his chair, then finishing me off by leaning over and smashing my neck, his hand a steel fist in those special fingerless gloves. Maybe it'll be a sniper with scoliosis. I don't care. I'm ready. I've lost my will to live. I'll turn on all the lights, every last PermaBulb™, and give them an easy target. I'll go out in a blaze of incandescent glory.

Culture Clash

Mr. *Whatever* from East Wajoo is sputtering and complaining about the overdue fines on the books he's trying to renew, this white paste forming in the corners of his mouth as he does that little "jat jat jat" thing they do when they're excited. It's enough to make my stomach churn, that and his breath, but all the East Wajooans have that breath, it's like pepper, feet and bad meat all wrapped together with garlic paste and fermented in milk, so I should be used to it since they bussed all these East Wajooans in last year and gave them welfare and library rights and they're always around. But it's hard to be, like, *eating* that breath, if you know what I mean, when they stand so close to you. Their custom, if you can believe this, is to try and speak directly *into* your ear—maybe in East Wajoo, bub, but not here!—so they settle for getting real *real* close (Stinkville, we call it, because they don't wash much either) and jabbering. The words come out in this rush of Wajooan and Funglish (Fucked Up English) and there's all this "jat jat jat" and "dullers" and "no!" and I just smile and nod and catch a quick breath when I turn my head to look at something on the counter, and I slide this form across the desk for him to fill out. It's our special form for the East Wajooans when they want to complain. They get to write their comments in Wajooan and then this guy from the Refugee Office comes by and picks them up and takes them to the Wajooan translator they hired (apparently some Peace Corps wannabe lady who teaches ESL at the Refugee Center) and she translates and sends it back to *us* and then we know whatthefuck they're *jatting* about and then the head *librarian* can take the comments and the complaints to the *arbitration council* and they can come up with a *solution*. There's a bunch of us, well, me and Clark and the Tooleys, and we know what the solution is, but it's not what people want to hear so we don't say anything to anybody about it. We just smile and do our jobs.

I tap on the form and tell him that he needs to fill it out and leave it with me and he gets this glint in his eye, thinking that he's going to just be able to walk out with those books he's got in that satchel, but that's not the way it works. The books have to stay here until the problem is resolved. He'd be better off just paying the fucking $2.15 and saving us all the headache and the money it's going to cost to process the complaint and get the translation and go to the arbitration council, but I can tell he's not going to go for it. I've worked with these people long enough.

"You have to give me the books," I say, and I smile, a sad "it's not me, it's the system, I'm on your side," kind of smile.

"Bookes?" he says.

I point to the satchel.

"Books. You have to leave them. I wish I could let you renew them until they figure this out, but it's the rule."

"No bookes," he says. "No."

I smile and I say, "Yes, books. You do. You have to leave them."

"No bookes," he says again. He slaps the satchel onto the countertop.

"Yes, *bookes*," I say. I reach for the satchel, forgetting about how it is with the East Wajooans, and I try to stop myself, but my hand is already on the canvas when he lets out this wail and says something in Wajooan and I pull my hand back like I'm scalded.

"Sorry. I'm sorry," I say.

"Jat jat jat," he says, then he glares at me, the hatred of a thousand years of little brown people like him getting fucked over and trampled by white people like me, this hateful, die-and-I'll-shit on-your-corpse glare coming out of his raisin eyes, and he makes this dramatic hand slashing gesture like he's whipping out some kind of Wajoo Kung Fu or something, and that's when I pick up the phone and call security.

Now, normally when security gets a call from the library they're thinking that we're just spazzing over someone trying to steal a bound copy of *Playboy* or something, and they take their sweet time responding, but it must be a slow day or something, because the double doors swing open in about thirty seconds and two of the University's finest come bustling through, one of them even has his hand on the butt of his pistol like he's Starsky or something about to draw down on a drug fiend.

Then this *scene* ensues. The cops are trying to talk to the guy, trying to get him to put the satchel back down on the counter, but he's not buying it, he's all worked up, and making these slashing gestures at me and then at them, and you can tell that the cops aren't digging it, because you know they've heard the stories about the Wajooans who eat that *stimtik* leaf and go whacko—there have been a few stories about cops ending up handcuffed in their own hardware, and sometimes naked—so they give him a count down, you know, tell him, "Sir, we're going to count from five to one, and then we want you to put the bag down and come with us." I don't know, maybe the guy can't count to five in English; certainly, it's a challenge to count *backward* from five. I mean, that's not exactly a frontline skill you need in another culture, right? So they start counting and he's jat jatting and slashing, and then he takes a step toward them and one of the cops pulls out a stun gun and zaps him, which is supposed to drop a 300-pound crackhead like a slippery baby, right? But no, Mr. Wajoo lunges and grabs the cop and now they're both doing the jittery jive and the second cop doesn't know what to do, so he pulls *his* stun gun and lets Wajoo have it and now both Wajoo and his partner do a little ballet leap and then hit the hard library floor like horseshit. Bam. Out.

Everything is silent. I'm like, holy shit, did I just see this? and people are coming from the other offices and the stacks and from the stairwells and the coffee shop, and we're all looking at this scene, and in all this nobody notices that Mr. Wajoo's satchel has been kicked over to the front desk, and so when the cop calls backup and two more roll up and they wake up their partner and put the cuffs on Mr. Wajoo and take him off, the satchel is still there. Henderson, my supervisor, comes out from his office in the back, and he doesn't see the cops, but he sees the satchel, which, according to Homeland Security rules—unattended suspicious bag in a public place—he's supposed to call in and we're all supposed to clear out, but, hey, this is a library, and people are always leaving their shit all over the place and if we called stuff like this in every time, we'd be a former library, and, besides, I know who it belongs to.

"What the hell happened?" he says.

I tell him the story, and I guess maybe I exaggerate Wajoo's aggressiveness just a bit, so there's no question about me panicking or anything.

"Where are his books?" Henderson says.

"I don't know. He had a bag. Maybe the cops took it."

He bends down out of sight and then pulls up the satchel and sets it on the counter in front of me.

"This it?"

"Looks like it, I guess."

He opens the satchel and tips it and this huge piece of butcher paper with strings wrapped around it slides out with a thwump on the counter.

"Why would he wrap up his library books?" Henderson says.

"Maybe it's their culture," I say, which is a running joke we have—okay, it's just me and Clark and the Tooleys—because, like, the Social Services people have been beating the whole fucking town over the head with this "different culture" slogan for like years now. Hell, they could eat stewed babies and it would be okay, because it's "their culture."

"Well," Henderson says, taking out his Swiss Army knife and pulling out a blade, "we can't check them in like this, so . . ."

And he slices the string and grabs a loose corner of the paper and pulls and the whole thing rolls toward me as it unravels and reveals a huge piece of moist, raw meat, what cut of what animal, I don't fucking know, but there are bones in there, and a chunk of skin on one end, and it's bloody and fibrous.

"Shit, Henderson, gross, man."

Henderson skips back from the counter like it's been electrified.

"Fuck."

He looks over his shoulder at the door, but of course security and the Wajoo man are long gone. Then he looks around to check if any patrons have seen the wad of meat. Dr. Demosthenes, a bald ancient former Classics professor the size of a dwarf who spends all his time in the library since his wife died, is looking at us from a few feet down the counter. He's got a gargantuan stack of books he wants to check out, and I'm thinking, what's the fucking point trying to learn shit when you're ninety? He smiles at us.

"Get this . . . get this wrapped back up and I'll check out Professor Demosthenes," Henderson says.

"Me? I didn't unwrap it. Why's it got to be me?"

"Because I'm your boss. Hello, Professor!"

I wrap that shit back up, I'm holding my breath, you know, my head to one side, and I'm using the gloves from the first aid kit. No telling what this shit is, and I ain't about to be the guinea pig who finds out by getting some kind of nasty virus or something because I wasn't supposed to be touching this stuff. But I'm not thinking about what this nasty hunk of meat is as I'm wrapping it in the butcher paper and then putting it in a plastic bag and then putting it back in the satchel. What I'm thinking about is the books Wajoo owes us. Where are the books?

Henderson comes over after he's checked the professor out.

"We have to get that shit out of here," he says.

"Call campus security. Tell them Wajoo Man can come get his package."

"Yeah."

So Henderson calls, and right away you can tell it's not a productive conversation, because first he's on hold for about five minutes, and then he repeats what he said the first time about three more times as he gets transferred around, and then he just listens and says, "Auh huh" about five times, and then he hangs up.

"Yeah?" I say. "So's he coming? Cause this shit gives me the willies."

"He can't. He went home. He had to catch his bus."

"Well, fuck, man, he's got to catch the bus back here and get this shit."

Then we see one of our friendly Social Service Assholes walking through the front door, and both of us say "shit" under our breath and smile.

"I'm here about the incident," he says.

He's one of those earnest, grey-skinned, humorless guys who look freshly shaven at four in the afternoon, probably carries an electric razor in his briefcase and his own toilet paper, grinds his beard down as he's sitting on the pot. Mr. Uptight.

"Incident?" Henderson says.

Mr. Uptight opens up a little notebook and reads:

"At approximately 2:15 this afternoon, Mr. Waal Aaal Uptalaa, attempting to inquire about the library's renewal policy, was insulted, his property confiscated, and subjected to an unlawful assault, apprehension, interrogation and detention."

I start to complain, but Henderson holds his hand in front of my face.

"That's a matter of interpretation," he says.

Mr. Uptight puts away his notebook and stares at the satchel on the counter.

"Of course," he says, "and it will all come out in the hearing. Right now we need to take care of Mr. Uptalaa's property."

"Sure," I say, and slide the satchel toward him.

Mr. Uptight looks at me.

"Are you the clerk in question?"

I want to tell him to clerk my nerk or something like that, because I fucking hate these guys and the way they've shoved all this Wajoo shit on us, but I just say, "Yes."

"And you were the one who took Mr. Uptalaa's property?"

"I thought he had books in it and was trying to get away with them."

Mr. Uptight gets his notebook back out, writes something in it, then tears out the page and lays it on the counter.

"This is Mr. Uptalaa's address. You'll need to return his property to him before nightfall."

I snort. "Yeah, right."

"Otherwise his honor will have been insulted, and we would have a very serious case of culture discrimination on our hands. I don't think I need to tell you what that could mean."

There it is again. Culture. These wobs think they can get away with anything by claiming their culture has been insulted.

"Discrimination?" I say. "Discrimination? Is stealing okay in their culture, then?"

"We're not talking about the incident with the books, but the confiscation of Mr. Uptalaa's property."

"We contacted campus security and told them that he could come get it."

Mr. Uptight makes a face like he's a teacher talking to some punk third graders.

"In Wajoo culture, when your property has been taken away without due cause, it is not the responsibility of the property owner to retrieve it—that would be Njantoopa, or "improper obsequiousness"—so the confiscator, that would be you, must do the returning, or risk insult to the property owner."

"Fuck that!" I say.

"Mr.—" Uptight says.

"Wemp," I say. "It's Taylor Wemp."

"You can do this the right way and save everyone embarrassment and time and money, and probably your job, or you can do this the ignorant, racist, difficult way and cause more trouble than you are worth."

"Racist?"

Any second I'm expecting Henderson to step in and start defending me, but he just stands there and watches while Mr. Uptight lets me have it. I turn to him, but he won't look at me.

"This is ridiculous," I say.

"It's the way things are," Uptight says, "whether you like it or not."

"Henderson," I say, looking at him, and I know that I sound like an insta-bitch complaining about the coffee in the break room or something, but he just gives me this "it's out of my hands" kind of look, and I just glare at him.

"So," Uptight says. He looks at his watch. "It's already been almost three hours. You'd better get going."

"What, am I on the clock or something?"

"It's a complicated social custom. Restitution must be made

before six hours have elapsed, unless there is some compelling reason for the property to be returned, in which case it must be returned sooner. In this case, there is a compelling reason, and that is that there is a ceremony tonight, and the property is needed for that ceremony."

I just laugh.

"You're shitting me, right?"

Henderson lets me go early, so here I am, in my rust bucket Subaru, heading across the river to Wajoo Town. Of course, no one calls it that to their faces. Everyone still calls it Smithville, but there hasn't been a Smith there in three decades. I'm going over the rusted out bridge in my rusted out Booroo and the sun is setting upstream like a runny egg yolk sliding off a plate, like it just said, "Fuck it," and is oozing out of sight, and I'm in a foul mood like I've never been. Up ahead, Wajoo Town festers.

A lot of immigrants, you know, they're colorful. They come from places where, I guess, there's not much to do but paint things in bright colors, wear clothes that look like explosions in a crayon factory, eat all these green and red vegetables and stuff. But not the Wajooans. The national colors of East Wajoo are, like, gray and taupe. Their national flag, which they just had made since they only ten years ago got free from Wajoo, which became West Wajoo, is supposed to be the national bird rising out of the morning sun over the ocean, or some shit like that, but it just looks like a lint sculpture in the fog. You see them on the street and its like watching shadows flit across the sidewalk in one of those time-lapse movies—clouds skipping across the sky, traffic lights flashing off and on, cars zipping then stopping then zipping then stopping. Wajoos sliding past your peripheral vision, stealth-walking.

I tried to get Clark or one of the Tooleys to go with me. Clark said, "Good luck," and the Tooleys just laughed. So here I am, slugging along like arterial plaque, this satchel of ungodly meat on the seat next to me, and I'm hoping I wrapped it up tight enough to keep the stink of some dead beast from penetrating deep in the upholstery. It's hard enough to get a date; I don't need the stench of death in my ride.

Uptight scribbled down some directions in addition to the address, but in the dim light, the writing on the crumpled paper looks like someone duct-taped a pen to a chicken, then cut its head off. I checked out the address on line before I headed out, so I toss Uptight's directions and follow the map I printed in the reference room.

You'd think that Smithville would be just crawling with Wajoos since they've been bussing them in for fifteen years, but there are other people around, people who have to be here, I guess, like city workers and people who run the shops and the police, and stuff, but everyone there who's not Wajoo seems to be a little uncomfortable. They don't make eye contact. It's like when you go into the porno shop and none of the guys wants to acknowledge that they're standing there in a public place with 30 other guys looking at full color photos of skanky women and unnaturally gifted men shooting manjuice all over them. *Don't look at me, I won't look at you. We're not here.*

I reach the street and here's my first problem: The three blocks of Clark Street are blocked off with metal poles, making it a walking mall. I see at the other end poles down there, too, so I can't drive around the block and hit it from the back side. I gotta park, then walk with this shit down who knows how many blocks, and it's getting dark.

I find an open meter at the curb, slide the Booroo in, make sure I lock all the doors. Not like I've got anything valuable in there, or that I would even mind it if someone lifted the 'Roo, but I don't want to be caught in Wajoo Town after dark without a ride. I mean, yeah, I know they're all supposed to be peaceful and everything, and the reason most of them came to America was to get away from the West Wajooans and the war and getting their asses kicked 24/7 while the world watched American Idol and ate Cheetos, but those stories about *stimtik* are real, and you can take any run of the mill good-guy Wajooan and turn him into a for-real fiend with just a couple doses of the blue weed. You see the stories on the news all the time: some average Joe Wajoo, been here for eight years, works as a draftsman for an architectural firm, stand-up guy, never late to the job, blah blah blah, one day goes home, some old buddies show up, tempt him with the demon *stimtik* weed, and the next thing you know he's put the baby in the deep fryer, skinned his wife and is hanging by his nuts from the patio banister. So I don't want to try to hoof it out of Wajoo Town after dark with the *stimtik* monkeys creeping in the shadows.

I hold the satchel like it's a grocery bag—no way I'm slinging it over my shoulder, that's for sure—and head to Clark Street. I can feel all these eyes on me from windows along the way, and I'm, like, people, it's *my* country and you're just visiting. It's dusk now and some streetlights start to blink on and I hear a siren somewhere back toward the river and the sound of *Klalaa Lim*, or Wajoo music, wafting from open windows. Whatever you want to say about the Wajoos, they can crank some pretty decent jams. It's like a combination of West African juju and Gypsy folk songs and Yemeni tribal music with a wicked beat. Not that I'm into clubbing and all that, but it is pretty hip stuff, and if I come across it on the radio, I'll leave it there for a few tunes.

So maybe I'm bopping a little, listening to the *Klalaa Lim*, as I schlep this satchel down Clark Street and turn sideways to get between the poles. It's part that the music is okay, and part that I want to seem like I feel at least a little comfortable here. *Stimtik* fiends can smell fear they say.

Clark Street is lined with row houses, three blocks of them stuffed together, and nearly every one is jammed with Wajoos. Some blacks still live here, and there are some Russians, too, you can tell from the Russian flags hanging in some windows, but mostly it's just Wajoos. Some kids are sitting on stoops, or playing this Wajoo stick and rock game in the street. Some of them are dancing to the *Klalaa Lim,* this traditional Wajoo dance where they look like zombies with the jitters, and some, you can tell, are waiting for the *stimtik* man to come with his bag of tricks.

I find the address. It's in the middle of the second block. The house has been painted a sickly green and the doors and shutters are brown. All the lights in the place are on and I can hear people jat jatting inside. In/out and then away to my car. I'll be back on the other side of the river in five minutes, ten at the max. I climb the stoop and ring the bell.

All the jatting inside stops and I hear some impossibly quick footsteps approach the door, and the door opens just a crack and this eye looks out at me.

"Jes?"

"I'm from the library. I brought the—the meat."

The door closes and I hear more jatting and some of it sounds excited and some of it sounds angry, and then the door swings open and there is Mr. Uptalaa, looking agitated and embarrassed and indignant.

"No bookes!" he says, then nods curtly and grunts. "Mmm? No bookes!"

"No books." I hold up the satchel and try to open the door.

Uptalaa shakes his hand, slices his hand at me through the door, turns and says a whole bunch of stuff, his voice going high, low, fast, slow, like he's talking to about twenty different people all at the same time, and people answer from all over the house, it seems. When he turns back to me, he is smiling like I'm the *stimtik* man and he's been jonesin' for three days.

"Come in," he says brightly. "Come in, Mr. Lieberry!"

In/out I'm thinking, just drop the meat and scat, but when I get in the foyer, Uptalaa is scooting down the hallway ahead of me

Culture Clash

toward the back of the house, the kitchen, I'm guessing, where all the noise is coming from.

"Come, Lieberry," he calls over his shoulder.

"I gotta go. My car is double parked."

But he doesn't answer and I'm thinking that I better not piss anybody off and cause any *more* cultural problems, so I switch the bag to my other hand and head off after him.

The kitchen is huge, but it's so packed with people you'd think it was an efficiency. The oldest person I've ever seen—hell, I don't know if it's a man or woman or what—is sitting at the far end of a big table smoking a little cigar and nodding at nothing, and there are kids scurrying all over the place and a woman who's probably Mrs. Uptalaa because he's jatting at her and slapping his hands together and she's rooting around in the refrigerator for something. There are some other men, too, guys who look like they've been working in the dirt factory or something, dressed in overalls and covered with a thin sheen of grime, and they're chewing and chewing and I'm sure it's not gum but our old friend Mr. *Stimtik* weed. They smile at me with blue teeth and one of them holds up a little sprig of leaves and winks.

Uptalaa clears a space on the table and motions for me to put the satchel down. I lay it between the two men and they nod like their heads are tied together.

Uptalaa says something to them and to the old lady, who smiles from behind her cigar.

"Okay, cool. Well, I gotta go. And you still got some overdue books, so you need to take care of that soon or you could lose your library privileges for six months."

I turn to leave and everyone starts talking at once.

"No! No go!" Uptalaa says, and comes around in front of me, smiling this aggressive smile that makes me take a half step back and wonder if something bad isn't about to happen.

The old lady starts jatting and jabbering, and everyone turns to listen to her. The cigar is flicking up and down in her ancient mouth as she talks, and ash is showering everywhere. Even the kids stop playing. When the old woman finishes, everyone looks at me.

"What?" I say.

Uptalaa starts talking to me very slowly, like I'm stupid or something, but it's in Wajoo, so I can't understand him. Just then I hear the thunderous flushing of a toilet, the running of a sink, and a door off the kitchen opens and this spacey-looking white dude the color of three-day-old canned tuna comes out and everyone turns to him. Uptalaa says something to him and the guy nods and pulls some *stimtik* out of his shirt pocket.

"You're the guy from the library?" he says.

"Yeah. I brought the meat, now I gotta split."

He looks at the *stimtik* a few seconds, selects a choice leaf, pops it in his mouth and chews.

"You can't," he says.

"Say what?"

I start to feel hot and these vague sensations of dread tickle my esophagus.

The tuna dude chews some more, nods his head, says something to old grandma. She laughs like a gutted hyena and he laughs along with her.

"Grandma says you have to stay. Have to do the *Duamalaat*."

Everyone around the table smiles at me, nods maniacally. I start backing toward the hallway.

"I don't have to do anything, man. I have to get home. I brought the meat, now I have to leave."

"*Duamalaat!*" Uptalaa says. "Very bad, no do *Duamalaat*."

"You're sort of obligated," tuna man says.

"Fuck *that*. I was obligated to bring that shit," I says, pointing to the satchel, and the Wajoos all suck in their breath and recoil, like I had just coughed up a loogie on the table. "But I ain't obligated to do nothing more."

Old Grandma starts talking and sucking in on the cigar at the same time, and I'm wondering how the hell she's doing that, and Tuna Man is nodding with her and chewing.

"Since you brought the *La'Umtra,* you are responsible for performing the *Duamalaat,*" he says. "Only you can do it. It would be sacrilege and discourteous and really bad luck if you didn't perform the ceremony." He purses his lips and nods, his eyes narrowed like he's really digging the gravity of what he just said. "Really bad luck."

That, I know, is my cue to get the fuck away from these people, so I brace myself, place one foot behind the other so I can execute a quick pivot, and then turn. And there, standing two feet behind me, is the most achingly beautiful girl I have ever seen in my life, sixteen, seventeen maybe, with dark, creamy skin the color of caramelized honey, perfect, completely white teeth, jet black hair shining in the dim kitchen light, puppy-brown eyes surrounded by completely unblemished whites, cheekbones that look like they've been carved by lasers, and a thin, straight nose that would put a pre-Raphaelite babe to shame. She isn't wearing a stitch of clothes, but my eyes don't leave hers.

"*Duamalaat,*" she says.

First, they give me this tart, frothy pink liquid to drink, then they bathe me. They—just the men—get me naked and put me in the shower, then they hose me down and rub me all over with lye soap scented with patchouli, then they put the *La'Umtra* in with me and have me hold it while they scrub it with a wire brush and then they rub it down with olive oil and hose me down again. Then they take it from me and wrap it in these huge, like plantain leaves or something, and they give me a loin cloth made of leaves, too, which they watch me put on, nodding and jatting, and then they take me into the parlor where there is a huge sheet on the floor with long white candles at the four corners and small bowls of incense burning some kind of cinammony-lemony joss sticks. I'm looking for the girl, but there's no sign of her, just a lot of movement in the other rooms, people talking, the kids laughing, and some humming kind of music that sounds like Grandma clearing her throat in time to some instrument. Tuna man comes in and tells me to lie down on the sheet.

"You gotta keep real quiet, or they'll have to start all over again."

"But—"

"Quiet," he says, like I'm a baby he's putting to sleep. "You just stay quiet and do as they say."

I'm feeling dreamy. It has to be the drink they gave me, but I'm not worried. I'm warm and kind of floaty. And I'm thinking about the girl and those dreamy puppy eyes and that these Wajoos are not that bad after all. They're people just like us. They just have a different culture, is all.

And then Uptalaa comes in, and he's holding the *La'Umtra,* and behind him is the girl, and she's dressed in garlands of flowers and her body is slender and honey brown and between the fully blossomed white flowers I can see her dark nipples like eyes staring at me and I'm thinking that it is a beautiful culture. Different, but beautiful.

She follows the old guy onto the sheet and he lays the meat on the sheet next to me and she sits down on the other side of the meat, and though I'm dreamy I can't take my eyes off her nipples, it's like they are looking right at me, hypnotizing me, and then, while the others come in and start playing this music—they have this two-stringed instrument and a little drum and some cymbals—I lie there and she smiles at me and starts rubbing the meat.

"*Umtalaa,*" she says, and the others say it with her, and she smiles at me and winks and rubs the meat.

"*Umtalaa,*" the others say, "*Umtalaa, Umtalaa, Umtalaa.*"

And there's this feeling of love and warmth and sharing and peace, and the music gets louder, though it's not much, really, considering the instruments they have, and I want to laugh, even though the leaves are chafing my crotch. I feel floaty and good. I feel like I am one of them.

And then I reach out and touch her nipple.

And it's like someone turned the world on its side and then set it on fire.

The girl shrinks back like I lit her up with a cattle prod, then throws her head back and shrieks long ululating shrieks of anguish and Tuna Man curses me and the Wajoos throw down their instruments and start jatting at me. Someone knocks over a candle and the sheet goes poof and there's suddenly a fire.

The girl disappears and someone comes and grabs the *La'Umtra* and I get up and people are running everywhere and jatting and they sound like they're angry and I know they're angry at me and the last thing I want is to get my ass kicked by some Wajoos, so I scramble up and weave my way to the bathroom, where my clothes still are. Tuna Man is yelling at me to stop or I'll ruin the ceremony, but I'm panicking, I'll admit that, and wonder nipples or not, I'm getting out of there. I knock somebody down running to the bathroom in the dark and I don't stop. When I smell the smoke, I know it's a matter of life or death and I'm not stopping for no one.

I grab my pants, but I can't find my shirt or my shoes. I stumble down the hallway and there's a light coming from the parlor that's wrong, too yellowish-orange, not a lamp or ceiling fixture, but a fire, and everyone else is yelling now and I think I smell burning meat.

The front door is locked with three deadbolts thrown, but I snap them all open as someone grabs my arm. It's Uptaala, and his face is all hard angles, like a badly carved totem. I don't even give him a chance, I put my hand on his forehead and push him back into the house and he goes down in an awkward heap.

I go down the steps as fast as I can take them feeling the floaty way I do. It's the first time I've been barefoot outside in years, and all I can think about is glass and nails and dog shit and hypodermic needles. But I have to get out of here, have to get to my car, and I push it all from my mind and just run. People spill out of the house and are yelling at me and soon other doors and windows are opening and the night is full of jatting and shrieking and some techno Klalaa Lim. I see the Roo, though, there in all its sickly brown rusted glory beneath a sputtering streetlight, and I know that all I have to do it is get there and everything will be all right.

Fucking Wajoos. What was I thinking? Nipples. Beautiful hair. A face like a supermodel. That fucked up cut of meat. It was all wrong from the beginning, but I couldn't see it.

I can hear them behind me, and I'm thinking, why don't they just leave me alone? What did I do? I did more than I needed to. I brought them their meat, didn't I? But I'm not about to stop and debate them about culture and civility.

I reach the Booroo, my salvation, and remember that I locked it up, so I reach for my keys in my pocket, and as I'm fumbling around the handkerchief and the change and some old sticks of gum I see, in the dim streetlight, something shining on the other side of the steering wheel, and my heart sinks and asks God for it not to be true. But it is, and there they are, my keys, two feet and one thousand miles away, dangling from the ignition switch.

I'm thinking I'll run, just haul ass to the bridge and over it back to town, forget about the car, let them have it, but who am I kidding? I don't have any shoes, my head feels like it's filled with helium and wet papier mâché, and I haven't been in shape since the eighth grade. Distance running is the national sport in East Wajoo. They name their kids after marathoners who run over jagged rocks and cactus in bare feet. And most of these cats have been eating *stimtik* all week long. They'd catch me by the end of the block, and that would just give them another thirty seconds to get pissed off. So I turn and face the foaming brown sea of Wajooans boiling toward me, their angry jat jatting filling the night, and I just wait. And from

Culture Clash

somewhere, wafting on the air, I hear the sounds of *Klalaa Lim.* Despite my situation, I feel my hands and then my feet moving to the beat. As I said before, all things considered, it's actually pretty cool music.

Sand Castle

One of the fathers, a poet, pauses, his hands protectively cupping a freshly set tower. He looks over his burnt brown shoulder at the sun's molten eye leering above the inland palms and searches for an apt metaphor. *It's as hot as—as hot as* . . . Words evade him, images dissolve.

"Hot," is all he manages, but the others don't hear him. They work.

The plumber, two towers away, swipes a meaty forearm across his brow and whistles. "Hot as a Kansas City hooker's belly on pay day," he says.

The policeman snorts. The minister reddens, but doesn't say anything. The service manager shakes his head and chuckles.

The poet, who has neither been to Kansas City, nor even *seen* a hooker, as far as he knows, nonetheless appreciates the image. He nods, picks up his bucket and goes back for more sand.

Mid-day, mid-week, mid-month; July, Naples, Florida. The beach stretches to haze in both directions. Beachcombers and sunbathers dot the sand like afterthoughts. The off-season. By Thanksgiving, the roads will be clogged with huge cars from the North and rental Mercedes driven by Germans and Italians and Swiss. The restaurants will overflow with perpetually tanned sexagenarians, trophy wives with outlandish breasts, golf pros and Cadillac salesmen. The beaches will teem with supplicants to UV radiation, most of them adults, the occasional Eurochild yelling at seagulls or floundering in the surf. The air will be freighted with expensive suntan lotions, sun block and perfumes, with cigarettes and cigars, and, over and above it all, the diaphanous aroma of cash.

But not now. Now it is July. An absence as real as the sun hangs in the air. The snowbirds have migrated, the Eurotide has ebbed. Minivans prowl the streets. Families from Akron and Cedar Rapids and Mount Pleasant and Scranton broil in the sun, offer their flesh to ravening mosquitoes, trudge through Everglades exhibits and check prices on menus before committing themselves to dinner.

Just past dawn. From the seventh floor hotel room terrace, the minister's young, pretty wife rests a hand on the railing, feels the ocean breeze through her nightgown. Below, gray waves silently slide ashore. On the horizon, gray of ocean melts into gray of sky. Her husband appears on the beach, arms swinging, bucket in one hand, shovel in the other. A man off to work. He turns and waves to her, swinging the shovel in wide, boyish arcs over his head.

It is the fourth day of their vacation and they have travelled no farther from the hotel than the short walk he is now making to where the others await. She waves back and watches until he is out of sight.

The elderly weatherman speaks slowly and loudly and uses broad gestures. The service manager diligently watches the late news each night. It is hurricane season after all. This weatherman is almost comical. Then the service manager remembers where he is and thinks of septuagenarians and octogenarians and nonagenarians and whatever you call people who are a hundred years old, straining to hear the forecast.

Old people like the weather, but it's funny, because mostly they just stay inside, especially down here. The house he and the family are renting, a block from the beach, is nestled among palm trees and poincianas in an old neighborhood populated by even older people. He never sees them outside, just sees their silvery heads gliding behind picture windows. It is for people like these that the weatherman speaks.

"Tropical Storm Eloise is slowly churning in the Gulf," the weatherman says slowly. On the screen behind him, the infamous counter-clockwise spiral of clouds twirls, and the weatherman moves his hands over the sinister vortex. The sequence is run five times. The vortex spins its way over the blue expanse, then spins again, again, again and again.

"All right with the clouds already." But the service manager watches nonetheless, and sees, at the upper edge of the screen, the appendage that is Florida.

"We're gonna have to keep an eye on ole Eloise," the weatherman says slowly, smiling.

Several children approach the working men, carrying their own plastic shovels and buckets, but they stop a short stone's throw away, watch the silent men dig out the third moat and reinforce the facing of the outer redoubts, then retreat and play listlessly at water's edge, looking back longingly at the largest sand castle they have ever seen.

The plumber's wife awakens to the sound of her children in the kitchenette. She turns over and sees the empty bed and is throwing back the covers before she has had a chance to swear.

The boys peer around the kitchenette wall when she flings the door open.

"Where the hell is he?" she says.

The boys, dressed for the beach, shrug.

"The beach," the oldest says. "I guess."

"Sonofabitch!"

They take breaks, of course. Lunch. Time with the families. A movie. But there is no golf and no half day fishing excursions with guides and six obnoxious salesmen from Youngstown. Time is important, especially now, Thursday, the end of the week near. And something else, too. Something out there. Eloise.

"Hey!" the policeman says.

Three teenagers have camped fifteen feet away, unfurling their towels, opening a cooler, setting their boom box to stun.

"Hey!" the policeman says.

The music from the box is surprisingly loud, obliterating the sound of the surf and wind.

"They broadcasting to Cuba?" the plumber says.

The poet shakes his head. The music sounds like people playing instruments while falling down a flight of stairs. He is a liberal man—a poet!—and yet this music is, is—*wrong*. He would never say this at the college where he teaches, where everything except outright public degeneracy is permitted, admired, celebrated, but here, among—among . . . He considers the others. What are they? What is he, with them? *Guys? Buds? Pals?* Are he and they a *Crew*? He doesn't know. But he does know that with them he can say the simple things he cannot say in school. He can be blunt, straightforward, honest. It is the work. The work has freed him.

"Okey doke," the policeman says, rising slowly and slapping sand from his hands. He approaches the teenagers.

The others glance at him as they work. The cathedral was a late idea of the plant manager's, but it immediately appealed to them and so now they are gamely trying to defy gravity and the qualities of wet sand to improvise some flying buttresses. Delicate work, it requires concentration. So no one sees the entire exchange between policeman and teenagers.

The plumber sees the cocksure walk across the sand. The minister sees the policeman stop three feet in front of the teenagers and hold out a hand of greeting. The poet sees the teenagers cast a semi-contemptuous glance at this barrel-chested stranger standing in their sun. The service manager sees the surly youths listen, immobile, as the policeman talks, arms and hands moving to the cadences of some story. The plant manager hears the laughter of the four, kids and policeman. No one sees the policeman walk back to the group. Everyone sees the three teenagers hastily pack up their gear and remove themselves to another spot on the beach, three hundred yards away. No one asks the policeman what he said.

The wives gather in the lobby of the high-rise hotel, where only two of the families are staying. There is precious little small talk.

"I say this shit's got to come to an end," the plumber's wife says. She is a small, intense woman with a brutally short haircut. She and her family are from New Jersey. "We been here four days already and everyday it's this sand castle foolishness."

She feels the righteousness of her cause and expects the other women to commiserate, but only the service manager's wife nods and says, "It's not healthy."

"I don't know," the minister's wife says, "I think men need to dream, to have visions."

"We're talking sand castles, honey," the plumber's wife says, "not world peace."

"It relaxes him," the policeman's wife says. "I get a chance to do some shopping. The kids like to watch."

The service manager's wife shakes her head. "I don't know. It's like everything else with him. Bowling, fishing, the Internet,

Y2K. He gets obsessed."

"At least this doesn't cost any money," says the poet's wife.

"They're wasting time," the plumber's wife says, "and that sonofabitch is always saying, 'Time is money, Linda.'"

She looks at the other wives and they just look back at her. What a bunch of sissies.

It is the policeman and the minister who build the first castle. The rough draft, the minister calls it, a set of towers and a wall before the tide eventually consumes it.

"I love this stuff," the policeman says, bending carefully to sit down beside the minister's tower. "Good for the soul."

By day's end they are joined by the service manager and the plumber. Seated on a train or at a bar or in the same section in a stadium, they would have little to say to each other. Here, at this place, where serendipity has placed them, something clicks and they work in the comfortable silence of old friends.

Onlookers congregate during the day. There are always kids careering and shouting at water's edge and along the periphery of the castle. Fitness walkers slow to enjoy the spectacle. Swimmers bounce in the waves and watch from offshore. On the third day a tour bus of Japanese students stops and for a few minutes the overcast afternoon pulses with hundreds of camera flashes. Word gets around.

The local tv film crew arrives on the fifth day. The castle is now a complex of buildings behind double walls and triple moats just beyond the reach of high tide. The cathedral has emerged as the focal point of the construction, not because any besides the minister and the policeman are particularly religious, but because, as the plumber says to the reporter, "It's a castle. Middle Ages, you know. Every castle had a cathedral. The Holy Catholic Church was pretty big." The others are inarticulate before the camera, shrugging, rubbing their chins, shielding their eyes from the sun.

"Why castles?" asks the perky reporter.

"It's just one castle," the service manager says.

"It's good sand," the poet says. "Good material."

The story will run on Saturday, the reporter tells the men, who are insouciant. Even if Eloise doesn't arrive, though, the story is doomed. The producer will look at the fumbling, inarticulate men and say, "This isn't news, this is weird."

Smiling, the weatherman says, "Tropical Storm Eloise has just been upgraded by the National Weather Service to Hurricane Eloise, a Category 2 storm with winds of 98 miles per hour."

The service manager sits in a lawn chair, a flash light across his lap, a thermos of coffee at his feet. The moon streaks the ocean with a shimmering stripe and the sky is so rich with stars that he laughs. He is not thinking of mechanics working on Subarus and Chevies, but of nighttime vandals, stumbling drunks, inquisitive dogs. He remembers a line from a WWI documentary, the French at Verdun. "They shall not pass," he whispers to the waves.

The sea grows angrier. Eloise, tracking north by northwest, moves toward the panhandle. Only the outer spirals will touch the coast, but that means seas of four feet by Saturday morning, the day when most of the families will leave.

They examine the impossible castle, its vulnerability, their folly. No one has brought a camera. They turn to the ocean, cast wary glances at the leaden sky. They put themselves between the surging waves and the high outer castle wall.

"Hey," the poet says. When the others turn to him, he simply smiles. Everyone laughs softly.

"What the hell," the plumber says.

They stand shoulder to shoulder, then reach out, taking hold of each other's hands, and face the water. They wait.

Sand **C**astle

By the Numbers

Freddie is running.

Running.

Frantic, leg-pumping, arm-swinging, for-your-life kind of running. The kind of running you recognize immediately as the kind of running you hope you never have to do.

Freddie is not in shape, and if you were watching, it would be obvious that he is not going to make it far. 75 yards and already he is in trouble, wheezing, gasping, spittle flying as he jerks his head to look behind him. The guys who are chasing him jog along, laughing, half in amusement and half in disgust. When they catch him, you would think, they just might kick Freddie's ass. Which is exactly what they do after about 120 yards when Freddie stumbles, slows and then stops, bent over, hands on knees, and retches. But first they wait for him to finish puking.

It is a "good" neighborhood, the kind of place where things like this never happen. In fact, it is surprising that people aren't somehow mystically attuned to the disturbance in the force field of sweetness and light that their subdivision exemplifies, aren't peeking out of their windows to watch this rare, half-block-long race drama. In other neighborhoods just a few miles distant, over the hill that way, or the railroad tracks the other, this sort of activity is practically a daily treat for the bored and the house-bound. The beat-down in the street. The beasting in the park. People would be providing a running commentary, pointing out the fine points of getting one's ass kicked in public. No one would be calling the police.

Which is not happening in this neighborhood, either. Maybe it's the time of day, around 2 p.m., that makes the noisy and spirited event silent and invisible to the neighborhood. Freddie tries to cry out when the first of the guys starts working him over, hoping someone hovering behind one of those sets of curtained windows might hear him, look outside and, shocked and sympathetic, call the police. But poor Freddie is winded, and these efficient, professional guys know how to render him inarticulate.

Freddie is blubbering and bloody in the time it would take for him to say, "I made a mistake, I'm sorry," but all Freddie can get out is "bwaw muwwwah muuuuhhhhm."

A car pulls up, and just as efficiently as Freddie has had his ass kicked, Freddie gets his ass thrown into the backseat of a late-model SUV, windows tinted to invisibility, and is driven away. A bird tweedles. A dog barks. A shadow moves behind a curtain. But no one calls the police.

LTK, which stands for Lorenzo the Killer, if anybody bothers to ask, but usually no one does, gives Freddie an ice pack for his face and a handful of pills. Freddie holds the ice against his nose, throws the pills in his mouth, then washes them down with the bottle of water someone throws to him and which he miraculously manages to catch one-handed and half-blinded.

"I—" he manages to get out, but LTK shushes him.

"Don't care," he says.

You might imagine, hearing the name Lorenzo, that Lorenzo is Latino, but in fact he is Dutch. At least, he says he is Dutch. He doesn't have an accent, to Freddie's ears at least. Freddie has only met LTK on the phone, after Freddie's friend, Larson, suggested the job and set things up. Meeting the man had been a surprising disappointment. A blonde Lorenzo with fingers like sausages, a voice like rocks in a meat grinder, and a vocabulary you wouldn't expect from a man who has "Kill" and "God" tattooed across his knuckles.

"Don't care, won't make any difference," LTK says. "A deal is a deal. All of us here?" He points to the men in the room who have beaten and kidnapped Freddie. The men all nod good-naturedly, as if to say, "just business, kid; you understand." "We all had our qualms, sure. Reservations, philosophical angst, uncertainties, fears. Some of us tried the old sliperoo like you did today. We had one kid, fuck, what was his name?" He looks around the room, but before anyone can answer, the name comes to him and he snaps his fingers, an act that sounds like someone slapping two kielbasa together. "Slink. Name was Slink. Slink, now he got beasted, set upon in a most outrageous fashion." One of the men whistles and high-fives another. Lorenzo chuckles. "Put him in the hospital for eleven days. He came out, saw things in the right light and has been doing big numbers since then."

"Monster numbers," says a man who twenty minutes before had been twisting Freddie's wrist at an obscene angle. The man holds his hands apart for emphasis, the space between those skillful hands meant to convey, Freddie guesses, a long series of digits and commas that added up to a number that was "monstrous."

The pills are catching in Freddie's throat, so he drinks more water. His mind is clogged with trash. Random shit from every corner and time of his life. If things were a little more orderly in there, he would have genuine cause for alarm, because it might really resemble a life-passing-before-your-eyes kind of experience. But it's not. It's like his mind is being ransacked by a crackhead, shit strewn every which way as the valuables are sought out.

Kurt Jose Ayau

"This whole affair has caused a backlog," LTK says. "Lots of unfulfilled contracts, which causes no little bit of disconcertion up and down the ladder. You can imagine the scenario. Like an accident on the freeway just backing traffic up all the way to the Golden Gate Bridge. So we need you on the job, doing the job, performing the job like we know you can."

Freddie has always wondered about the full ramifications of "we." Freddie has wondered about many things since Larson explained the deal to him. At first, it was a lark. A joke. A joke regarding a significant amount of money, but still a joke. Some fucking joke.

"It really isn't an automatic operation, contrary to what you might think," Larson had said. "People have got these ideas." He had stopped to make spirals with his hands to suggest the wild thoughts of the uninformed. He had been kind of manic that night, feeling good on something. But that was Larson. Happy-Go-Lucky Larson. "But it's really a managed process. People have to make decisions, be accountable. It's complicated and you, I guess, you get weirded out at first, but you have to remember, if not you, then somebody else. The work, like the world, has to go on."

"Larson said if it wasn't me, it would be somebody else," Freddie says, finally feeling the pills clear. In about twenty minutes he should be feeling much better.

"Metaphorically, sure," LTK says, "because, eventually, it's *always* someone else. The world turns. Because the job has to get done. But when you sign up, you sign up for the duration."

"How did Larson—"

"Larson's on the list," LTK says.

"What?"

"He didn't tell you?"

"No. No, he didn't!"

Freddie is feeling sadness and rage and confusion.

"Hey," LTK says, "everybody gets on the list eventually."

"Yeah, but," Freddie says. He can't complete the thought.

LTK shrugs. He reaches out and pats Freddie's unbruised shoulder.

"You'll do okay, kid. You take a day off—which in itself causes problems, exacerbating the backlog; I'm getting calls, but I can handle it—but after that you get back on the job and knock the numbers out and everything's on the up and up."

Freddie, staring at his shoes, says, "Do I have a choice?"

And everybody, including Freddie himself, laughs.

Freddie sits at his desk with a bottle of wine and two commercially-rolled joints. Larson said it always helped him get "creative," which, Larson said, *LTK* said *"they"* liked. If you put things on automatic pilot, stuff gets predictable, "they" weren't happy. The system slows down. You don't want to be known as someone who just goes through the motions. Yeah, the numbers will be there, but what will they *mean*? "It's a fine balance between Renoir and paint-by-numbers. But you gotta give 'em Renoir. You gotta give 'em Magritte every once in a while."

He uncorks the bottle, pours some wine. Some expensive French stuff, which he can almost afford now, just like he can almost afford this new Honduran weed everyone has been raging about. Good wine is something he has just discovered. Good wine is pretty amazing when you've been drinking Gallo and Almaden all your life.

He gets out the new map, the city/county combo map that he has to use since his territory crosses back and forth over the boundary in several areas. To his mind, it is inexcusable given all the attention paid to productivity and efficiency and numbers and what have you, that territories aren't more cleanly delineated. But there are reasons for everything, he knows. *Old* reasons, but reasons. And besides, he doesn't get to ask those kinds of questions. He shouldn't even be thinking about questions. Thinking about questions led to his aborted 200-yard dash the other day.

He uses the compass to draw in his territory again. The old map is becoming illegible, dotted with ink smears, wine splotches and roach burns, but he does his best..

He drinks half a glass of the wine in a big, wasteful gulp, not savoring the taste, just looking for the effect, does a small hit off the Honduran. Two joints is probably overkill, from what the Rumanian kid down on the corner who sold it to him said, but better to have more than you need than to have to run out halfway through the job and try to score at four in the morning. He puts on his glasses and looks over the territory. Picks a few intersections, gets out the directory. Runs his fingers up and down the cheap, nearly translucent paper, lets his imagination do a few laps.

Makes his choices. Long-term, mid-term, short-term and immediate. Keeping a flow going. Making decisions. Making art.

"Someone's gotta do it," he says to the air above his head. He knows that *someone* is listening. "Someone's always gotta do it."

"They" allow it, because, *"they"* say, it provides perspective, but too much can make the whole process morbid, obsessive, addictive even. You don't want addiction, because then you start getting what LTK calls greedy, and that can throw things way out of whack. So they allow it, but someone's always checking the numbers.

Freddie takes a cab to 14th Street at 11:30. He's feeling—judicious. The word unfolds in his head. Judicious not as in, he's a wise man making wise choices, but in the sense of an almost righteous kind of high. The Honduran weed is not overrated, he has decided.

He takes an outside table under the awning at the new French-Brazilian restaurant, orders some escargot and espresso, checks his watch, looks at the road. The fog has burned off and a delicate blue sky is taking shape overhead. On the other side of the street, heading up the hill in his direction, a young mother leans into a stroller.

The incline is steep. She's in relatively good shape—several days at the gym, lots of walks with the kids—but she still can't manage to take off those last fifteen pounds that her husband insists he doesn't mind, but which she knows he secretly abhors, hence the various sites she's discovered saved under his Favorites/Humor folder, none of which are humorous. The cellulite that won't go away, the flab around her belly. If she had gone Caesarian, would it have been easier?

Freddie's order comes. He scoops the escargot out of their buttery-garlic shells, sips the espresso, but not too noisily so he can hear.

The delivery van is a quarter mile away, sounding closer because of the metal-on-metal squealing that has been eating away at the driver's brain for the past week, he'll tell anyone at the shop who will listen to him, but they're backed up a good ten days with repair work, thanks to the moron manager who pissed off the best mechanic and is now short an experienced hand. Everyone tells him it's just the brakes, but it's not the brakes, he knows. He's heard bad brakes before, and this isn't it. It's not the brakes.

It isn't the brakes.

Freddie knows.

The van comes down the hill, signaling to make a left, slowing for the turn. From the left, like a small dog darting into traffic, a gust of wind blows a paper grocery bag halfway out into the street. The driver, startled, cuts the wheel hard right, curses the bag, then yanks the wheel back left to make his turn.

The mother pushing her stroller has the light against her, so she has stopped and is looking down at the baby, cooing, as the van, squealing that awful sound, swings left, then lurches into the side street in front of her. She doesn't get to say any last words. Just baby-soothing noises, nonsense, gurgles.

The driver feels the truck sway, then lunge as the front axle snaps. He only manages to say "shit" several times.

Freddie sees the four-hundred pound truck tire, rim and all, leap spinning into the air. The truck continues around the corner, slaloming and smashing cars to either side in the narrow side street.

The stroller, its wheels locked seconds before, sits immobile as the young mother is crushed and flipped backward, her mind, synapses firing a "we're dying!" SOS, flooded with sunshine in a kitchen fifteen years ago, when she told her parents that she was in love and thought the boy was going to ask her to marry him.

Other people at the outside tables have half-risen from their seats, gasped, groaned, invoked the name of God. The truck tire has bounded beyond the crushed woman into the main street and is still bouncing wildly downhill toward oncoming traffic.

11:37. Freddie does not move from his seat as others rush from the restaurant to cross the road to the woman, the baby, the truck driver who has climbed up out of the van that has pitched over on its side.

Freddie watches from his table, but he wants to run across the street with them, to also stand helpless at a safe distance and stare, simultaneously horrified, but unable to look away. He wants to be able to grab someone's sleeve, tug at a hem, and say,

"A work of art. A work of fucking art."

Kurt Jose Ayau won the Tartt First Fiction Award with this, his first, collection of stories. Kurt teaches at Virginia Military Institute in Lexington, VA.